Come Apart

Roger Colby

This is a work of fiction. Names, characters, places and incidents either are products of the author's imagination or are used fictitiously. Any resemblance to actual events or locales or persons, living or dead, is entirely coincidental.

The opinions in this manuscript are solely the opinions of the author and do not represent the opinions or thoughts of the publisher. The author has represented and warranted full ownership, and or legal right to publish all the material in this book.

This book may not be reproduced, transmitted or stored in whole or in part by any means, including graphic, electronic, or mechanical without the expressed written consent of the author except in the case of brief quotations embodied in critical articles and reviews.

For the mistakes we make, and the grace that covers it all.

1: Startup

As his eyes slowly opened, Michael felt the springtime sunlight flood into his brain on a wave of pain. He lay belly down, sprawled on a soft carpet of green grass, his arms and legs splayed out as if to welcome a chalk outline. He squinted his eyes closed again, catching one of the green blades in his eyelid and then blinking in reflex. He felt grit between his teeth as he began to wonder what he was doing here but more importantly who he was.

A strange ringing echoed in his ears, much like the after effect of firing a 44. magnum at close range without ear protection, but over the din he could somehow make out chattering high pitched voices. One of them formed the shape of a sentence.

"Mister, are you OK?"

He wondered if this statement came from inside his throbbing head. Rolling over on his side to face the direction of the sound, he raised his hand to shield his eyes from the brutal sun. Silhouetted there, her yellow dress dirty, tiny nose running, stood a small girl with unraveling pigtails. She grinned at him, two teeth missing.

He tried to speak to her but could not form the words.

"What are you doing here?" she asked, her pitch a roller coaster. "Are you sick?"

He managed to rise to a sitting position, but that only tightened the vice grip on his skull, causing him to feel something roiling in his stomach. Again he tried to speak, but his words seemed jumbled, cross-wired. He could only produce gibberish at which the little girl's thin eyebrows rose.

He was mildly aware of a string of warm drool escaping his bottom lip.

The little girl giggled, and that was when he heard something from a deeper, more adult voice nearby.

"Don't talk to strangers!"

"Oh yeah," said the little girl. "Sorry mister." And she toddled off, the hem of her gingham yellow dress bouncing along.

He rose to his knees, shielding his eyes from the sun without much success, and as the white washed world faded to familiar colors he saw that he was near a small playground, rusty swing chains squeaking, children laughing. A few of them squealed as they descended the blue cyclone slide. The pain in his head, a titanic jack hammer, pounded away with each beat of his heart.

He raised his hand to wipe his brow and discovered that he was holding a small silver chain tightly in his fist, and a disc shaped locket hung there, swaying back and forth. Somewhere in the distance a small dog wailed and barked.

The playground looked vaguely familiar to him but he could not place it, like seeing a faded picture of a childhood residence. He managed to stand, feeling something like the symptoms of vertigo, and staggered over to place one hand on the rough bark of a nearby tree in hopes of ceasing the psychedelic madness of the spinning ground. It helped slightly, and he found that watching the children play caused the unnatural motion of the earth to subside, but his stomach retained the feeling of dread, gurgling and bubbling.

His vision blurred, then focused, and he saw a vibrating line of something that could only be called red static moving across the ground from his feet, a sparkling circle, small bolts of red lightening squirming out of it, washing over all of the children and the playground equipment as it moved quickly away from him, causing the children's features to warp and shift, their faces becoming oddly scrambled. And then it was gone, the children somehow not fazed by the phantom ring.

He blinked his watery eyes.

Something in his head, a voice that was not his, told him to go home.

Where was that?

He could not remember his name much less where he lived, but somehow he knew this playground, this part of town. His eyes scanned the area, looking out past the playground to a nearby street and a row of uniform houses, and he inexplicably knew that they had been built in the 1950's. A faded blue sedan crawled by, its driver a blonde woman, her name lost in a fog, her right hand vigorously texting on a phone and the other trying drunkenly to stay on the road. Something in Michael caused him to grunt out a short laugh.

He shambled to the fence that separated the road

from the playground and opened a latch on the gate, wobbled through, closed it behind him. The sidewalk, small tufts of green grass poking up through the cracks, led away to a main street and more traffic, and he saw the woman's yellow signal light blinking as she turned onto the main road and then sped off to the left.

"Bye, mister!" shouted the little girl.

He spun his head on a swivel and the small child was waving a skinny little arm, her doll-like hand a blur. This is when he noticed two women sitting on a bench on the other side of the playground glaring at him, their eyebrows furrowing, their lips moving slowly, one of them reaching into her purse to produce a cell phone, the other clutching her handbag with both hands as if it were a sack of pirate gold.

He ignored them, a dumb mechanical grin altering his face, and then turned to walk down the cracked sidewalk. He appeared on the main street, or so he thought, and he vaguely knew that if he went along it far enough that he would find his home, but couldn't remember which way. Something like electric mist was starting to clear in his mind and he was seeing more and more familiar landmarks floating out of that haze, but he still could not remember his own name.

As he rounded the corner on a row of small town red-brick store fronts, someone slammed into him nearly knocking him to the ground. It was an older man with oily, dirt caked clothes, reeking of unwashed hair and sour alcohol. Two brown eyes stared out of all of that dirt and the old guy grunted a curse.

The ring of red static exploded from the vagrant this time, but did not affect either of them, warping only the surrounding pane glass windows and other innocent bystanders.

"Watch where you're going, dummy!" the transient growled, his voice strained.

I know you.

"Ss…" was all the amnesiac could manage. The old man, his face ringed by an unkempt halo of long gray hair and peppery beard, the top of his head bald but with liver spots, pushed past him to walk toward the barber shop across the street. The old man paused to look back as if he had forgotten how to speak, his near toothless mouth agape, and then scurried away.

Sickness overwhelmed the amnesiac.

His stomach began to roll and bubble and his throat closed up. He found a door to a storefront and upon pulling it open, listening to the small brass bell announce his entrance, he smelled fried bacon and saw many red and white checked round tables around which several townies ate their breakfast. As if on cue, they paused their lives to stare at him, each face a puzzled mask. Dark murmurs were heard as he staggered toward the sign at the back that read "restrooms", found the men's room and rushed inside to dry heave into the cold porcelain toilet. Rising to the sink he pressed the button on the single chrome spigot, plunging his hands beneath the cool water and then shakily rinsing his face, its coolness soothing the pain in his head.

That is when he looked in the mirror.

He jumped.

A man he did not recognize stared back at him. He had close shaven dark hair, a balding area on top, a shaggy dark goatee ringing the mouth and wrinkled circles around hazel eyes.

"Who are you?" he mumbled, his tongue finally working. "And where are you?"

A knock at the door startled him and he took in a sharp breath.

"Hey in there," came a woman's soft voice. "You OK in there?"

Her name... What is her name?

"I'll be right out," he said, grabbing a handful of paper towels from the stainless steel dispenser and wiping his face. He used the paper towel to pull on the bathroom door handle and propped it open with his foot as he threw the wadded towel in the trash. A young woman wearing a jade button down shirt beneath a grease spotted off-white apron stood in his way.

"Michael," she said, her cobalt eyes wiggling back and forth, studying him. "You been out all night again? You gotta stop doin' that. Bad for your health."

Michael. I think that's...

"I...I don't know."

She held an orb shaped pot of coffee in one hand and a pen in the other, a large yellow plastic flower attached to the end of it. She pointed over her shoulder with the flower.

6

"You want a cup of coffee? Might do you some good."

He nodded, wiped his mouth with the back of his hand, and when he did a spark of red static jumped to his lip, causing him to jerk backward awkwardly. He still held the chain and locket in his left fist, so he hurriedly shoved it into his back pocket as if hiding contraband.

She led him to a worn chair at a table toward the back of the restaurant and brought out a cup of black coffee, a small bowl filled with cold disposable cups of creamer and a glass sugar dispenser with a dented chrome lid. He found a spoon in a paper napkin along with a fork and a knife and instinctively poured cream and sugar into his coffee, wondering if he liked coffee.

Yes. He really liked coffee.

He watched the waitress serve other customers and then his eyes widened slightly.

Judith. Her name is Judith Rigby.

He straightened his right leg and reached into his front pocket where he found a set of three keys on a rubber keychain bearing a picture of a cartoon roller coaster that spelled out the words "Frontier City". He also found a wadded up ten dollar bill and in his other back pocket opposite the locket a wallet with a few business cards for businesses he did not recognize. No driver's license or identification other than one of the business cards which had something scrawled in pencil across the back of it. He couldn't make it out because apparently some of the graphite had been rubbed away. It looked like a phone number.

Michael. Michael...Pros...Prosper. Yes, that's it. Prosper.

He sat quietly for some time, sipping at his coffee, watching Judith do her lonely job. As he sat, he started to recall the bittersweet taste of the coffee, the sounds in this restaurant, the smell of good food, and Judith's kind face. He supposed she wore that kind face for everyone.

A memory jostled, but as if someone had crammed it into his ear.

Oh yeah, her husband died. Couple of years ago. Brain cancer. She has a little boy...what's his name? Dawson! Oh that kid is a brat.

Lost in thought, Michael didn't notice Judith appear next to him and slide the green and white check stub across the table.

"Um...all I have is this ten," he said to her, pulling the crumpled bill out of his pocket again, that mechanical smile appearing. His keys fell on the scratched, hard wood floor.

"It's ok, honey," she said, the corner of her mouth twisting. "It's on the house. You go home and get some rest."

He did not say another word, only retrieved his keys, rose to his feet, and silently brushed down the grass stained t-shirt he was wearing. He exited through the front of the restaurant, this time not many people acknowledging his presence, and a few of them waving nervously.

Where is home?

He glanced above the door to a sign that read Kendall's, written in some strange forest green balloon animal font, and then he saw red and blue lights flashing, reflected in the pane glass of the door.

2: Warning

Michael turned, a grimace forming on his face, and there before him parked at an angle against the street was a white unmarked midsize pickup, the lights on the dash flashing blue and red. Michael blinked and then squinted into the glare.

A thick bodied man, a square jaw beneath a ten gallon Stetson silver belly hat, mirrored aviators obscuring his eyes, approached slowly, one hand resting firmly on the butt of his holstered Glock.

"Michael Prosper," came the deep voice of the officer, his brown and tan uniform, the shiny brass badge, somehow out of place with the snake skin boots. "You must have messed it up something awful last night. Heard you had a little mishap over toward the playground this morning. Don't tell me you was out drinking last night after all the bad choices you've made up 'till now. You'd think you'd have learned your lesson."

Prosper could not speak. He only winced and put his hands to his sides, trying not to seem threatening.

"Just checking on you," said the officer, a grin forming, one incisor slightly crooked. "Have you checked in with your boss, or are you going on home for a good rest?"

Michael glanced quickly at the meaty hand resting on the holster and decided that this lawman's offer of a ride was not exactly a suggestion. He nervously walked to the passenger's side and popped the handle, sat in the blue vinyl seat, and before he could reach for the restraint the officer was magically plopping down next to him behind the wheel, his big hat nearly scraping the ceiling of the cab. In moments they were backing out into traffic and onto the road, driving slowly down the main street as if in a parade of shame, onlookers stopping to stare.

"I had some kind of episode," Michael blurted out, trying to help his case a little. "Didn't mean to scare anybody."

"Well you did scare somebody," snapped the officer, turning his hard edged face toward Michael with a strangely swift motion for such a large man. Michael could see his own unfamiliar face reflected in each lens of the mirrored aviators. "Nearly shocked the socks off Suzie and Mabel Karnes. Didn't even see you lying there 'til you stood up. You wanna tell me how you ended up taking a nap in the park?"

Michael looked at the officer's big farmer hands again, this time noticing a black spot beneath the right thumb nail. A tiny paper calendar stuck to the dashboard told Michael that it was April.

"Don't really know, officer," he stammered. "Can't really remember."

The man's blocky face turned slowly toward Michael again and then back toward the road.

"Officer?" he chuckled, his face turning red, that crook-toothed grin forming again, his deep laugh a gravelly wheeze. "You ain't called me that in a while, Prosper. Can't you even remember my name? I need to take you to the clinic?"

"No," Michael replied softly, timidly, cringing in his seat. "I just—"

"Well shoot!" said the officer. "Darnell Norris! Pleased to meet you, boy! Dat gum, Michael, we played ball back in the day before your life went to pot. 'Fore you started drinking heavily and screwed up your life. Don't you remember nothin'?"

"Heh, yeah. Guess so."

No. Not really.

"Listen," said Norris, his voice lowering to an even pitch, his words falling like frozen water vapor from his near lipless mouth. "I'm not gonna truck with no deadbeat probation violator. You done considerable well until now, so don't blow it. I'll be watching you pretty close from here on out. I don't know what you got into last night, Prosper, but I'll find out...and when I do...well we'll see, won't we?"

Silence fell on them except for the noise of the road and the blood pumping through Michael's ears.

"If you keep things up, you'll be living under a bridge before long. Is that what you want? Living under a bridge? What the heck happened to you, man? You used to be a great guy. Had a great girl, too. What was her name? Kalila?"

Michael thought about the silver locket.

"I... I don't really remember anything before I woke up there in the park, honest Darne---"

"Sheriff," he grunted. "You can call me sheriff. Elected to the title, I suppose you can call me that, bud, since you put yourself on that side of things."

Michael's face felt warm as the dizziness slowly

returned and somehow he couldn't stop thinking about the silver chain in his back pocket. He could feel it just against his skin, a small knot pressing against him. He thought about reaching for it, but then looked at Norris's Glock.

Michael closed his eyes and sucked in a breath. He silently turned to his right to look out the window, watching as they turned onto another potholed blacktop road, and then he heard another deep rumbling chuckle coming from the officer. He suddenly imagined a large linebacker tackling him to the ground, grinding a thick knee into his sternum.

"Shoot, man," said Norris. "I'm taking you on up to your place to get some rest. You check in with Burke at the shop, see if you can't keep things together…at least this time. Don't wanna lose that fine job you got."

Michael could feel the bile rise to his throat as he tried not to glare at the man. The sheriff simply ignored him, touching the front brim of the grey Stetson as they passed a couple of teenage girls in a light blue Volkswagen Golf.

"Here we go," said Norris as he turned the wheel with the palm of one of his large hands, the truck rocking to a stop. "Looks like this is you."

Michael couldn't open the door fast enough, feeling the air pressure rise within the cab.

"Hang on now," snickered Norris, giving Michael pause. Michael could not shut the door of the truck. It was as if he were under a spell. "You need anything, anything at all, you let me know, you hear?

Don't be a stranger…because I… *won't* be."

There was a long pause. A small dog yelped somewhere.

"You can shut the door now," said Norris with a grin, eyes mirroring two tiny images of Michael.

Michael closed the door carefully, holding his breath, and then watched as sheriff Darnell Norris put his truck in reverse, backed out onto the road and then flicked his hand in a polite greeting, that predatory smile on his face, and sped away.

Michael stood still for a moment, listening to the truck engine rev and then fade with the other sounds of small town life. He turned to see a faded blue apartment building, rusty railings on the stairs, and reached in his pocket to find the keys that he hoped would open one of the doors.

It would be like nervous roulette.

3: Insertion

As the room faded from black, there was a faint hum, the smell of antiseptic and bandages, and blurry lights unfolded like bright origami stars.

Sitting in a blue vinyl chair beside him was a woman, dark red hair, glassy green eyes, box of tissues in her lap, mouth opening as he reached up with one hand to brush across his cheek.

"Danny?" she gasped. "You...you're awake."

He tried to speak but could not. He shakily wiped a string of drool from his mouth, feeling embarrassed in front of this strange woman.

"Took a nasty bump in baseball, son. Doctors said it was a concussion but the CT scans and MRI came back negative. So lucky."

Son?

He was lying down mostly, his head and shoulders propped up by a few pillows and there was brushed metal railing on either side of him. He looked at the back of his hand where a clear tube felt cold and uninviting, taped there with smooth white tape. He wanted to scratch at it, pull it out.

She sat quietly for a minute, as if to think of her next words carefully, then she leaned forward and touched his leg and he twitched.

"It's ok, Danny," she soothed. "Doc said you'd be a little out of it when you came to. Just normal he said... why are you looking at me like that?"

"Like what?" he asked, surprised that his words

came out of him so quickly. It was as if he did not form them, as if there was an electronic speaker somewhere in his head.

"Like that," she smiled. "Just there. Danny are you ok?"

He stared at her for a moment and then looked toward a window that was propped open slightly, noticing the baby blue curtain flutter as the wind caught it, and he did not know his own name.

"Who are you?" he asked mechanically.

Her eyes drew from a new well of tears as she sank back into her blue vinyl chair. She pulled another tissue from the box on her lap, the act of which seeming to shatter her resolve.

"Danny," she sobbed, barely able to produce words. "I'm... I'm your mom. Kalila Steren. We moved here from San Diego after your dad... You know, to be next to where I grew up, to start over."

He nodded, looked at the back of his hand again, then displayed a painted on smile. She saw the forced nature of it and it caused her face to fall. His was more of a grimace than a smile, a dull expression of utter confusion. He honestly did not know his name, whether or not this woman was truly his mother, or where he was for that matter. He was lost, like the wind blowing through the window was lost, blowing through from some place unknown to this room and eventually to other places unknown.

"I'm pretty hungry," he said, his other hand playing with the clear plastic tube. "Can I get... some...some tacos? Not the hard shell kind but the street taco kind with...with pulled pork?"

Somehow he did not know his own name or if this woman was his mother, but he did remember the taste of food and that he wanted it badly. She smiled, dutifully almost, and stood, approaching an antiseptic formica counter on one side of the room where she retrieved her grey purse. She turned back to smile at him and that was when he saw something that looked to him like red static flow out from his bed in a wave that moved across the room and across the face of this woman calling herself his mother, warping the features of her face briefly and then echoing out to the walls. Small bolts of amber lightening shot out of it, feeling along the floor and walls as it went, and then it was gone.

"Did you...?" he asked, his voice strangely echoing in his head.

"What? Tacos. Street tacos, right? At least you can remember that much. Guess that's a good thing."

"No," he said, blinking. "Did you see that?"

"See what?" she smiled, her eyes a little too wide for a genuine smile.

He sat silently in the bed and she patted his shoulder.

"I'll go get those tacos," she said, rising, fidgeting with her purse.

"Maybe you'll remember something else if I get something more familiar than this God awful hospital food. Be right back."

She left him, and he could see the wind pick up the curtains and blow them around as the opening and closing of the hospital room door changed the air pressure. He could hear the little machine attached to the hanging bag of fluid cycle more of it into his hand and into his blood stream, and that was when he started to think that this woman might indeed be his mother...but he still wasn't that sure.

In moments he took a deep breath, and then his eyes closed again and he drifted off to sleep.

4: Defragment

Michael stood motionless in the parking lot of the apartment complex trying to remember if he was indeed home. The compact apartments, their meager faded and peeling light blue walls rising out of a parking lot full of divots was home to a scattered collection of low-end used automobiles, a few of them with paint primer on the fenders or doors. If he didn't remember living here, at least it started to feel like something he had seen before, like a faded memory of home or like revisiting a childhood playground.

He pulled the keychain from his pocket and nearly dropped the wadded up ten spot. Scratching his balding head he walked sullenly to the familiar building and tried the first door he saw: apartment 122. The key slid easily into the lock and then wouldn't turn, but that was when the door popped open, jerking the keys from his hand. They hung in the door knob mockingly.

An older woman appeared, her hair black and streaked with grey, her skin dark brown and aged by the sun.

"Que pasa?" she grunted, then smiled, a silvered tooth visible. "Ah, mister Prosper. You need something?"

"No," he said, calmly reaching past her to pull the keys from the door. "I...I know this sounds weird, but I kind of forgot where my apartment is."

She laughed, shouting something back behind her in Spanish then turning back to face Michael with a squinty eyed smile. Michael noticed two little brown eyed girls peeking out from behind her turquoise dress.

"You live right above us, Mister Prosper," she laughed again, a wheezy smoker's laugh. "You need to stay out of the bars."

He couldn't remember going to a bar.

The door shut as quickly as it had opened, and Michael found the nearest set of stairs, shuffling his feet slowly to the second floor without holding the hand rail and he soon arrived at the apartment directly above.

Marta is her name…yes, that's it. Marta Gonzalez. 222.

The last number on the door was missing a rivet so that it tilted ever so slightly. He tried the door and when it opened he recognized that it was his apartment simply from the familiarity of smells. The memories flooded back to him. The carpet needed cleaning, someone had once smoked a pack a day here, and the Glade plug-in was working very hard to mask all of that. It was a small one bedroom with a kitchen and dining room and a darkened living room littered with one old couch that he remembered buying from a thrift store, a battered, red, ten speed bike leaning against the wall, and a dirty plate he had used at some point to eat a meal and then had abandoned in the sink.

An aching began in the backs of his calves and he

sat down on the creaking couch to rub them. He felt a tightness in his legs that was uncomfortable and strange. He wondered what he had done to cause this pain, chalking it up to getting older. He lay back against the lumpy pillows on the couch and closed his eyes, but all he could see behind his lids were images of the day: the red static, the warping faces of the children, his reflection in sheriff Norris's aviators. Something deep within the underground lake of his mind bubbled to the surface, a phrase that echoed through a darkness that shrouded who he was, a compulsive need to find some alcohol.

The phone rang, an annoying electronic sound, shaking him out of his thoughts.

He did not move at first, his eyes remaining closed, listening to the high pitched ringing of the cordless phone, and finally he crossed the creaking linoleum floor of the kitchen to answer it.

"Hello?" he said, his voice timid, quiet.

"Where in God's name are you, Michael?" came a gruff voice over the phone, not diminished by the tinny nature of the light static produced by the speaker. "If you don't get down here to the station in five minutes, you're fired."

5: Creche

Danny awoke again in a room adorned with posters of bearded Boston Red Sox players and logos, the smell of something salty cooking somewhere and the warm wet tongue of some small dog licking his nose.

The dog smelled strangely like plastic fishing worms.

It stood on the bed with two front paws on his shoulder, its wooly fur black and white, the damp whiskers surrounding its stunted snout where a pink tongue flicked in and out. He pushed it away carefully and small sharp teeth nibbled at his fingers and a tiny metal heart attached to a collar jingled like a small bell. The little dog bent its head down to grasp a tattered yellow tennis ball in its mouth, nearly too big for the limits of his breed.

Shih Tzu.

It was a voice inside his head, speaking as if it were teaching him the word, and it did not sound like his own.

Something was shaking the bed, and when he rolled over to his left to see what it was he saw another small dog. This one was long with short legs and wiry yet curly gray and copper fur, its head trapped inside of a white plastic cone which prevented its attempt to join its friend on the bed. It began to whine and yowl impatiently.

A faint smile cracked his parched lips.

"Are you feeling better?" came the voice of the woman who called herself his mother. She stood at the door. "I was wondering if you were going to wake up. Slept all the way through the ride home."

He could not manage a response, only stared at her and tried to smile again.

"Thirsty," he coughed. "Could I have some water?"

"Oh yes." Her eyes widened, her face lighting up. The sight of her smile registered deep within his heart as a primal comfort. "I'll get that…breakfast, too. Bacon and eggs — lots of fruit…apples or pears?"

"Pears…Yeah, pears.".

You are safe here. Don't worry.

She darted out into the hallway, back to the kitchen he supposed, and he grabbed the small Shih Tzu and set him carefully on the floor. The little mop of fur jumped back onto the bed like a fuzzy leprechaun and grabbed the ball again, staring at him with two black shark's eyes under a mop of grey-black fur, his whiskers forming a funny little dark mustache. The other impish dog was preoccupied with its cone and why it could not bite at the bandage wrapped around its mid-section.

He stood, and because he was feeling a little dizzy, he reached out to grab the wooden newel post on his bed. It felt loose in his hand, probably needed to be fastened to the bedpost. He stood silently, getting his bearings, his head swimming, and he shuffled out the door and down the hall in his boxers and t-shirt. His mother was shutting the door on the dishwasher. He could smell her perfume mingling with dishwasher detergent.

"Breakfast is ready," she chimed, that smile again. "I've called the school and your teachers will be getting all of your makeup work together. I'll go pick it up later after work if it's ok. You just lie in bed or in the living room and watch TV until I get back. Doctor says it's ok to watch some."

"Ok," he parroted.

She sniffed, then used a brown dish rag to wipe down the counter tops, her red-brown hair in a pony tail, her form fitting athletic clothes accentuating a trim figure.

The Shih Tzu, now at Danny's feet, growled at him, dropping the worn tennis ball on the tile floor, his pink tongue flicking in and out of his mouth with a strange lapping sound as if he were trying desperately to lick his wet stumpy nose. Ignoring the small dog, Danny sat at the table. A surreal feeling swirled in his stomach, one of not knowing who he was and feeling that all of this was foreign.

The table was set for one person, a glass of juice and a blue plate with scrambled eggs and bacon, small slices of yellow pear. His mother circled the table and kissed him lightly on the cheek.

"Gotta go, Danny," she smiled again, the smile covering something that to him seemed slightly dark. "I'll be back after work and we can talk about when you might feel up to going back to school. Coach says you should just lay low for a while...take it easy."

"Sure," he mumbled, using his fork to poke at the

eggs and two slices of bacon. The pears glistened. "I'll do that."

"Alright, then," she sighed, hesitating as if to say more, but didn't, only: "See you later."

And she bent to kiss him on the cheek again, her lips feeling somehow strange and clammy, the sweet scent of her perfume in the air mingling with the minty aroma of toothpaste. When she walked out the door, locking it behind her, he rose, moved to the window and parted the front curtains to watch her walk down a sidewalk, pass a "for rent" sign that had fallen over and climb into a small red car. He turned, took in a deep breath, let it out, and decided that the eggs and bacon needed to be eaten. He might not eat the pear.

After breakfast he walked down the hallway, the walls adorned with pictures of people he didn't know except for himself and his mother, and as he crossed the threshold of his bedroom a wave of that strange red static flowed out from him, across the bed, and then down the hallway behind him. This time it made him nauseous and he felt the eggs and bacon come back up and spill onto the hardwood floor in front of him. He watched in horror as the two dogs, sitting beside one another in his room, were covered with the red static, their features scrambled, and then when it cleared they spun and spun, chasing their tails as if mad, yowling and shrieking.

He fell to his knees, the world spinning around him, and then the light faded, the smell of something acrid and hot moving through the air around him.

A cool black cloth enveloped his body and he felt the world melt into darkness.

6: Menial

The ten speed needed grease on the shifters.

Michael pedaled down the cracked sidewalk that ran in a line along the storefronts. He passed a pharmacy, a clothing store and several other mom and pop businesses on his way to the Sinclair station on the other side of town. Some of them looked familiar. It had taken several minutes for his boss, a gravelly voiced man named Burke, to accept that Michael had forgotten how to get to his place of employment.

"There will be hell to pay," Burke had shouted before he had silenced his end of the line with a crackle of static and half uttered profanity.

As Michael rushed along, the warm spring air causing his eyes to water, he understood that he was probably going to be in for a bad day at work.

He approached an intersection with the usual set of stop lights and pressed the button on the lamp post to cross the street. He waited, and then when it was time zipped across, nearly clipped by an over-anxious driver who honked at him and then raised his finger of defiance out the window. Michael ignored it. One more problem to deal with on this strange and awful day. He could see the green dinosaur of the Sinclair station and started squeezing the brakes on the bike, hearing them squeak and complain to him. A red hatchback sat in front of the garage and the rolling panel garage door was being raised by a short stocky man with thick black hair tied back in a pony tail. The squeal of Michael's brakes seemed to call to the man who then spun around, locking on Michael with eyes that seemed to fire laser beams.

"I honestly don't know why I keep you on here, Michael," he growled, wiping his hands on a red rag and stuffing it in the back pocket of his faded blue coveralls. "I mean, really."

"I'm sorry, Burke," said Michael, remembering his name from the eviscerating phone call earlier. "I'll get right to work."

"Missus Anderson here has a slow leak in her front right tire and is already late for work because of you. Get in there and fix it. I told her you'd do it for free 'cause she had to wait."

"Yessir," Michael replied, sort of timidly, and then suddenly knew that he'd have to go through the tool chest to find the silver impact wrench. Somehow it came to him, not necessarily where he was as much as what he had to do to fix a flat, as if it were muscle memory. He rolled the chipped blue hydraulic jack under the front axle of Mrs. Anderson's little Ford Fiesta, twisted the handle, gave it a few pumps and before long he had the wheel off and was spraying it down with soapy water from a spray bottle and looking for any air bubbles.

This procedure moved quickly, methodically, and before long he had helped Mrs. Anderson, a woman he didn't know but who talked to him like she had known him for years. He faked most of the conversation with her, feeling like he was lying, all the while wondering how he knew so much about changing flats.

As he watched Mrs. Anderson get in her little car and drive away, touching up her lipstick in the rear view mirror as she drove, he heard a grunt next to him and turned to see Burke staring at him.

"When you're done taking your break," he hissed. "Some little kid spewed their breakfast all over the bathroom in the back. Take a bucket and get it cleaned up."

"Yessir," said Michael instinctively. "I'll get that."

He found a wheeled bucket and a dirty mop at the back of the garage, filled the yellow plastic receptacle with hot water and Pinesol and wheeled it out the side door to the back of the gas station where the door to the men's room had been propped open with a broken piece of cinder block. He went to work, slopping the water logged mop onto the sick and swirling it around. Once he had cleaned up the mess, he heard the bell from the air hose out front which told him that a customer needed service.

He didn't know how he knew this, but he just knew.

As he wheeled the bucket back to its home near the water spigot, he saw three young men pile out of a lowered purple GMC on the other side of the single pump station, probably a '68 or '69 by the looks of it.

How do I KNOW this?

One of them, a kid whose satin blue athletic shorts rose out of the sagging waist line of his black, faded jeans pulled a cigarette and a lighter from his front pocket and proceeded to light up right in front of the gas pump.

"No smoking within five hundred feet, kid!" shouted Michael, his voice catching in his throat a little, noticing that he had put his hands up like he was being robbed. He moved quickly to the front driver's side bumper of the truck.

The bloodshot grey eyes of the teen jerked up at him as the kid put the lighter away and took a drag off of the cigarette. His flat billed baseball hat, looking like he just purchased it moments ago, sat cocked to the side. The eyebrows furrowed ferally.

"Done it before," he said, his voice tinny and raspy. "What's to stop me now?"

Michael felt a presence behind him and the smell of rancid body odor and turned to see one of the other boys standing there rubbing his nose and leaning on the hood of the truck.

"Got somethin' to say, gas pump Joe?" he giggled. "Just wave at us and shut your hole. Pump our gas, old man."

Michael backed up against the pump, feeling cornered, but Burke appeared on the other side of the truck, his face sour and sweaty. The little punk with the cigarette put it out in the palm of his own hand, eyes squinting shut.

"Get your butt back to the garage, Mike!" screamed Burke. "I ain't payin' you to lollygag!"

Michael shuffled away, listening to the giggles of the boys and feeling their dagger-like words about his level of intelligence and questionable parentage slicing through his heart.

Shouldn't let it get to me. Just kids. Just like I used to be.

"Sorry Burke," he said, waving and trying to smile. Burke turned and walked back into the main structure of the station, a sad little convenience store. Somehow Michael knew that Burke had an office at the back of the store over behind the main counter and suddenly remembered flashes of long, one-sided conversations, of mostly Burke yelling.

Michael looked at the black and white clock when he entered the garage again, a small metal cage covering the numbers. It was only 9am.

It would be a long day.

7: Visitor

The sun dipped down below the squat buildings and ugly storefronts as Michael pedaled his ten speed back to the apartment. Throughout the day he had settled in to his place, so to speak. His name, his face, the backs of his hands, all felt more and more comfortable with each grueling hour at his post in Burke Isaac's employ.

Yet something within him, something down deep in his stomach wanted to get out of there.

For now he decided to just let the wind blow across the top of his head, speed home along vacant sidewalks and back streets until he reached his apartment that somehow smelled like home.

There it was, the light blue walls rising up out of the potholed pavement, the rusty chain link fence around a needs-to-be-mowed playground with fallen swings and a sign on the gate which read "Keep Out". He casually wondered where the children who lived in the apartment complex played.

Hefting his bike clumsily to his side, he ascended the stairs, his feet shuffling on the concrete and rusty metal steps as he went, his eyes wearily gazing at the numbers on his door, and then he noticed that the last number two that had fallen had been nailed back in place. As he fumbled with his keys Michael wondered if the same person who had fixed the number had ever thought about the playground.

When the door opened, the smell of home hit his

nostrils, a smell of bachelordom, lackluster cleaning habits and mildew from somewhere near the air-conditioning unit. The carpet, a filthy shade of brown, stained with cigarette burns here and there even though Michael could not remember smoking, felt surprisingly good on his feet when he removed his shoes after parking the bike just inside the door. He closed and locked the portal to his humble domicile, pulled off his shirt to reveal a physique that was nowhere near his days as a high school athlete, and opened the copper colored refrigerator to satisfy his aching stomach.

What he found caused him to do almost a cartoony double take.

Lying in perfect rows on one of the shelves, in place of where there might be a gathering of various perishables, was a perfectly stacked row of microwaveable burritos and behind that an expertly arranged circle of yogurt cups of all flavors and primary colors.

A short chuckle emerged from his throat as he took one of the burritos, filled a glass with water from the sink, popped the burrito in the microwave, and stood by the humming device while he waited for the ding.

He opened a cabinet near him, finding a stash of random junk and old papers, and gleaming there, a jewel in the darkness, the silver locket he had carried from the park. Reaching inside with a trembling hand he found the small silver chain. Pulling it toward him, the small round locket swung out toward him, dangling there silently. He used a thumbnail to open it, and within he found the picture of someone he knew, but couldn't place the name. Strangely, he didn't remember placing the locket in this cabinet.

The microwave dinged and he put the locket back, his hunger overtaking his curiosity, touched the burrito to see that it was not ready, restarted the microwave and shuffled over to the sectional corner he apparently used for a couch, then plopped down to find a remote for the small television.

Click.

The little tube television snapped to life, a small wood cabinet job, at first displaying a pop of static before snapping to life, and there was Andy Griffith talking to Barney about why he should not be in the Christmas choir.

Click.

Lucy was trying to pack all the bonbons in her mouth.

Click.

"You rang?"

Click.

Every station he landed on was broadcasting some type of old program, all of them in black and white. He stood to look at it closer, wondering if he had satellite or some other device, but the small box beside his television was only a converter that translated digital signals. No cable.

Ding.

Setting his glass down he stood to grab his dinner,

and when he opened the microwave he heard a thumping knock at the front door. He tottered over, and holding his warm burrito firmly in his fist he peered through the peep hole in the door.

A set of wild eyes made Michael pull his face away quickly from the peep hole.

Thump-thump-thump.

He recognized those eyes. He looked again and saw the man stand a little farther back, the shabby fish-eye lensed image of the homeless man he had seen just after waking in the park the previous day. He looked away again, and then set his burrito down on a lonely coffee table that stood by the door.

Thump-thump-thump-thump.

Maybe he'll go away.

Michael backed away from the door, stood still, wondering if the man was still there, decided to step forward, and looked through the peep hole again.

Gone.

He turned, picked up his burrito, and as he moved toward the kitchen again saw a ragged shadowy shape standing just outside the window over the sink, ringed by the light of the security lamp in the parking lot.

Michael screamed, dropping his food on the floor and stepping on it accidentally, feeling the warm refried beans and meat squish into his sock.

"Go away!" he shouted. "I don't know you! Why are you following me!"

The man's eyes widened, two bleach-white golf balls in the darkness, and then the shabby shade ran, the sound of heavy boots clomping down the stairs. Michael drew the navy blue curtains closed and little particles of dust could be seen in the overhead light of the kitchen lamps.

He went to the phone, picked it up out of the cradle, held it to his head, put it back, picked it up and then after looking around through some papers found the number for the police on a calendar with a picture of two dachshund puppies above the month of April.

He dialed it.

"Noble Police Department," came a woman's voice on the other end.

Silence, then: "Hello?"

"I—I want to report a vagrant," he stammered. "Just outside my door. Don't know the guy, he was just knocking and…"

"Sir calm down. I'm sure there's a logical explanation for —"

"No way! This guy was staring in my window and I don't know if he's still out there. He was knocking for several minutes."

"Sir what is your name and address?"

"Well…My name is Michael Prosper and I live at the…well I live at…"

Dead air.

"Mr. Prosper…Michael. Have you been drinking?"

"No. No I haven't been drinking. This guy was at my door and —"

"Now just calm down, Michael. We'll send

someone right over and check on you if that's ok. Are you feeling alright?"

The words started to form on his lips but he couldn't quite produce the sounds. In the silence he could hear breathing on the other end of the phone.

"Michael," came a familiar voice, a voice that boomed, sounded like it was meant for radio. Michael knew who it was.

"Yes sir."

"Michael if you've been drinking you need to tell me so that I can help you. I ain't gonna throw you in the clink if you're in your own place, but if you get out and cause a ruckus I'll sure as shooting lock you in the tank. You want I should come get you anyways just to make things safe?"

The world was spinning.

"No, no, no…just had a bad dream, that's all. Heh. Just a bad dream."

Thump-thump-thump.

"Just a bad dream, that's all, really. Sorry to bother you all. No need to come by. I'll just go back to bed."

"Anything we can do to help, Michael?" said the sheriff, his hand obviously muffling the phone on his end to tell someone something. "We ain't gonna have no camping trip in the public park again are we?"

"No, no. Going back to bed."

Thump! Thump! Thump!

Michael hung up without saying a word, his voice locked in his throat, his chest feeling tight. He slipped the socks from his feet and crept over to the door again to look through the peep hole.

There he stood, looking into the hole as if he could see through it, the shabby old man, his grey hair falling across his shoulders, his beard a matted mess, his bald pate a liver spotted leopard pattern.

"I need to tell you about the town," came the old man's muffled voice through the door. "There's a desert just outside of town. Gotta see it! Gotta see it!"

Blue and red lights appeared behind the vagrant's scraggly head, haloed, and the old man turned, spun slowly, carefully as if in pain, then skittered down the stairs and out of view.

Michael opened the door.

The patrol car below let out a loud whoop, just one, and then two policemen, not the sheriff, climbed out to confront the vagrant in the parking lot. Michael walked forward, out onto the second floor walkway, over to the rusty iron railing and peered down on the scene below.

The vagrant was throwing up his hands, shouting something about "fake people" at the police officers as the two uniformed men leaned against their car and folded their arms, the blue and red lights flashing as if a disco had opened in the slums. As the vagrant moved away, mumbling something unintelligible, one of the officers looked up at Michael and waved before they both returned to their car and sped away.

Michael went back inside his apartment, dead bolted his door, and after cleaning up the mess he made on the kitchen linoleum, ate a second burrito before finding his unkempt bed where he lay awake for several hours before sleep finally overtook him.

8: Guest

Danny's eyes flicked open at the sound of an echoing voice, the soft voice of his mother sounding as if it emerged from deep within a cave.

"Oh, Danny," she said, kneeling down beside him on the floor. The lights in the room hurt his eyes as he pushed away from the carpet and sat next to his mother.

"I must have blacked out," he mumbled. "Was out for a while."

"I just got home," she brushed his hair back with her warm hand. "You slept here all day? Oh no, you lost your lunch right here and must have laid in it. Let's get cleaned up. Want me to run you a bath?"

He looked at his t-shirt, matted with sick.

"Ugh...no. I'll take a shower. What time is it?"

"It's nearly eight. Maybe I should call the doctor and see if we can get you in tomorrow morning."

He cleared his throat.

"No, no. No more doctors. I just want to get on with my life. Go to school. I think I need to go back to school."

She felt his forehead and a smirking grin fell across her face.

"I think I need to take you back to the doctor for sure. You mean you *want* to go back to school?"

He smiled and it felt strange to do so.

"Yeah, mom. I guess I need to get back, right? Bits and pieces of things are coming back to me, but I'm

40

pretty sure I'm supposed to be in school. What am I, seventeen?"

She stood and then helped him to his feet.

"You hungry?" she asked.

He nodded.

She left him and he fumbled around in a dresser drawer to produce some fresh clothes and after a long hot shower he could smell something savory wafting down the hallway.

Later, a hamburger steak, mashed potatoes, green beans, a large glass of sweet tea and a slice of key lime pie all went down quickly and then he sat with his hands in his lap, leaning against the back of the dining room chair as his mother quietly cleared the table.

Things seemed right for a change, the fog of confusion was lifting, and somehow he began to feel that the things around him were familiar and real, not a fantasy or on some other planet.

"Mom," he asked. "I... have a friend named Grant...Grant —"

"Arterberry," she said. "Yeah, he's been calling your cell. Texting mostly. Wanting to know how you're doing. I can have him come over if you'd like and it's not too late."

"Yeah, that'd be cool. My phone. Where is it?"

She rolled her eyes.

"And here I thought I'd actually get to talk to my son without him thumbing away at his phone all the time. I guess it's back to the way things were."

She went to the black refrigerator, magnets

holding pictures of their lives all over it, and soon held a white iPhone in her hand. She gave it to him with some disdain.

He thumbed it awake, and saw that he had about four text messages from Grant:

yo wat up. hear u got 2b gvn bath by 2 nurses lol

Next.

dude we all frkd abt u geting hrt. hope u get well soon

Then.

hole school is asking bout u. came by but u out cold. nurse look like my dad

And.

praying at church. youth grp all ask bout u. Im like ur publicist 4COL lol

Danny replied with a curt message, with just about as much grammatical acumen, and then placed his phone on the table. In seconds it whirred and he read the message.

brt

"Looks like he's on his way, mom."

"Great," she said, drying the last plate. "You guys shouldn't play any XBox because doc said you don't need the visual stimulus or whatever."

"That's ok, mom. We'll just catch up."

She put the plate in the cabinet.

"I guess I could make some cookies. Bet Grant hasn't had any of my snicker doodles. Haven't made them since we moved here. Bet he'd like them."

"Yeah, ok," he grinned.

In around ten minutes, and after Kalila insisted on running the steam mop on the hardwood, they heard the sound of twin tail pipes and then the light from headlights washed across the opposite wall through the windows. A knock at the door.

"You look like somebody stomped your guts out," said a dark-skinned teen with short black hair, a generous dollop of mousse. He put up his hand and then swiped it down when Danny didn't return the gesture. Danny gently grasped the teen's forearm.

"Grant?" he asked, his eyebrows rising.

Grant looked at Danny, a confused grin across his face, then looked at Kalila and then back at Danny.

"That's what my momma calls me," he laughed. "Man, what's up with you? You suddenly go all short term memory?"

"Yes, Grant," Kalila replied. "He has some residual amnesia. Doctor said that it would wear off in a few days or so. He has the weekend to get things together. Thought you could, you know, jog his memory."

"Memories don't jog, Miss Steren, but I'll see what I can do."

Noticing Grant was still standing on the threshold, Danny pulled him inside and shut the door behind him. Grant nearly danced to the living room recliner and in one swift motion sat, pulled a lever on the side and then propped up his muddy boots. His face fell as he looked at the fresh tracks that went from the front door to his comfy resting spot.

"Sorry Miss Steren," he said as he rubbed his nose.

"Grant..." she started. "I guess it's ok. I'll take those boots of yours."

He kicked them off and she caught them, placed them near the door and then proceeded to go to the kitchen for a broom. Danny sat slowly down on the couch adjacent to Grant.

"Your mom is awesome," Grant beamed, a strange fascination. "How much...I mean... how much do you remember about things?"

"Not much. Just bits and pieces really," he said, looking down the hallway at his mother, then whispered. "I sort of know my mom even though it's still kind of weird. The house is familiar, but still not. I know I'm supposed to go to school and don't know how much time I've missed, and I feel that nagging feeling that I have something to do...just can't place it."

"Homework, bro. State testing. Gotta go prove to the testing company that you know all the stuff they want you to know so that you can graduate and get a real job. Not like our teachers went to college for that, right?"

They laughed a bit as Kalila began sweeping up the dirt that Grant's boots had scattered across the floor.

"You want I should get that, Miss Steren?" Grant said, his legs pressing down lightly on the recliner foot rest.

She turned, one eye winking, corner of her mouth turning up.

"Whatever, Grant," she chuckled. "Nice of you to offer though, even if you weren't really serious."

"Love you, too, Miss Steren."

The boys snickered for a bit and after that died down, they heard Danny's mother giggle softly.

"You gotta call Kallie," said Grant cocking his head back and looking down his nose. "She's worried sick." Eyes widened. "Sick!"

"Kallie?"

"Yeah, man. Oh snap! You don't remember your own girlfriend? Wait till I tell her that, then maybe... Hey, dude if she and you are done then I could move on in if you don't mind."

Short pause.

"Look bro," said Grant. "You probably have that school dance pic from last year you could pull out of your wallet or did you lose that when you ran into that foul ball post?"

Images flashed through Danny's head of a baseball falling...falling...and his glove up to catch it as he ran down the third base line and then something hitting the right side of his face...then cold darkness.

"Just a sec," Danny said, and he hopped up.

In a few minutes he returned with his wallet and reached in to produce several business cards, a movie pass, a couple of twenty dollar bills and a few photographs of his mother and himself, and then one crisp photo of himself and a girl in a beautiful electric blue dress, her hair the same color as his mother's, and a smile that one of those models wear when they have been taking pictures for hours and their faces hurt.

"Yeah, that's her," said Grant, watching as Kalila

disappeared into the kitchen. "Honor student, captain of the debate team, one step away from head cheerleader and totally fooled by your obvious fake charms."

When Danny looked closer at the picture, holding it with the tips of his fingers by both hands, the face looked familiar, and then he remembered the soft texture of her hand in his, her warm breath on his neck, and suddenly the picture animated in his mind to reveal eyes that sometimes rolled up and to the left when she was frustrated with something he said.

"How come she didn't text or call?" he asked.

"No idea," shrugged Grant. "Prolly cause of her troll face father. You remember him? Guy's the sheriff, man. Hyeah yeah! He's all crazy about keeping her from being a baby momma... even though..."

Grant looked left and right, lowering his voice to a whisper.

"...You know you and her... you know..."

"No I don't know. Whatever, man. I don't think I'm like that."

"Not like what? Straight? Dude, take another look at the picture—"

"You boys want some iced tea?" came Kalila's voice from the kitchen, and then she appeared at the doorway, large smile, iced tea glasses tinkling and sloshing.

"Yeah, Miss Steren," Grant said, his face shifting. "Love that stuff! Like awesome in a glass... Do I smell cookies?"

She handed the tea glasses to the boys and they held them as if they were delicate wine flutes. The sweet smell of vanilla floated around them as they sat back in their seats and drank the bittersweet goodness.

"Hey look, man," said Grant between gulps. "It's your stupid Shih Tzu."

The black and white mop of a miniature dog stood on the hardwood floor, staring at the two of them, his black eyes barely visible behind the wiry hair protruding from the top of his head and face.

Danny winced.

"Can't really remember his name," he said. "Like William or something."

"Walter!" Grant called, and the dog ran to him, jumping up onto the chair next to his right leg and lying down. Grant leaned back into the recliner, setting his tea down on the coffee table just to the left of the coaster.

"How could you forget the name of your own dog, bro," Grant chuckled.

Danny lay back on the couch and faced Grant, wondering how he could have forgotten such a weird name for a dog. As if in a dream, Grant slowly reached out and placed his hand on the dog's back. Danny watched the dog, his eyes transfixed on the grey and black and white mop, and suddenly teeth began to appear as the dog's lips peeled back in a threatening display. Grant, oblivious to this, his hand stroking the dog's fur, was taken by surprise as Walter spun around and clamped his tiny teeth down on

Grant's wrist.

Grant wailed, his arm twisting and writhing, sitting bolt upright in the recliner, and then there was a clanging metal noise and a rattling of dishes in the kitchen as Kalila darted into the living room.

"Get this thing off me!" Grant screamed, and Danny shot to his aide, grabbing the dog around the chest, feeling its strangely rigid body beneath that shaggy rug of fur. It was as if the dog had clamped onto Grant's arm and then simply died.

"Walter?!" Kalila shouted. "No! Bad dog!"

But the dog was not listening. Danny held a stiff dog in his hands, a dog that was not warm but cold as if it had been dead for hours, and the blood was running down Grant's arm.

"Get like a screwdriver or something!" Danny cried.

Kalila stood for a moment, her eyes darting back and forth, and then she ran to the kitchen, opened a drawer and brought back what Danny had requested, a flat-nosed screwdriver with a yellow transparent handle.

"Here," she said, almost a whisper. "Is…is Walter dead? What happened to him?"

"I don't know," Danny offered. "He just went crazy for some reason…all crazy."

Danny pried the dog's mouth from Grant's arm, and when he did the dog fell away and stayed in the position he was in when he first attacked, legs stiff, body tense, mouth agape, the little white edges of the pupils visible beneath the black wiry fur. Kalila ran back to the bathroom and came back in seconds with a first aid kit and some peroxide. After about ten agonizing minutes, she realized that she was not equipped to treat Grant's wound.

"Grant I need to take you to the clinic," she stammered.

Grant, holding a wad of gauze on his arm, nodded in agreement. Kalila looked at Danny and sighed heavily.

"Danny you have to stay here," she said. "Doctor was serious about bed rest, and if you're up there with us you'll not be doing that. You ok here?"

"Mom, I wanna come with you…"

"Stay here, Danny, please. I'll call Grant's mom and she can come get his truck later. We have to go."

Danny's lips curled.

"Yeah…yeah ok," he said. "Ok I'll stay."

"Let's go, Grant," she stammered. "Go get in my car and I'll be out in a sec. It's gonna be ok."

Grant went out the door, but before Danny's mother kissed him on the forehead and left to take his friend to the clinic, she grabbed little Walter, wrapped him in a blanket, and ran out the front door slamming it behind her.

Danny fell into the couch, his mind spinning with what he had just seen. He'd have to go see Grant soon…even if he didn't really remember ever knowing him.

9: Glitches

Michael forced the wide push broom across the floor of the garage, little pieces of candy wrappers and other detritus drifting across the concrete. Business was slow today.

The noonday heat made the pavement outside wiggle and wave. Michael wiped yet another teaspoon of sweat from his brow with the back of his hand. The blue-gray coveralls he wore, grease stained and soured, were quickly getting soaked despite the large fan sitting on the floor of the garage, its whine trying desperately to drown out the loud phone conversation that Burke was having in the small storefront that made up the other half of the gas station.

"Yes," Burke's voice was firm, authoritative. "I will speak to him about this immediately. You have my word on that…don't worry ma'am, I'll take care of it."

Michael continued to sweep the garage floor, staring out the large bay doors that were rolled up into the ceiling to help with the heat. A few cars puttered by on the street but none of them needed gas or a flat fixed or a limited variety of stale snacks and lukewarm sodas.

The phone slammed down near the cash register, its old fashioned bell ringing slightly in one solitary tone. Burke appeared just outside the bay door.

"We need to have a conversation," he said, his

hands behind his back. Michael had a brief thought about something that happened in high school years ago involving the principal, but that image faded into the starkly cold reality of his grumpy boss who now looked more grumpy than ever.

"What is it, Mr. Isaacs," said Michael timidly, his voice cracking. He knew what would come next.

"It appears," Burke's head cocked sideways. "It appears that you have messed up again with yet another customer. Now I told you that you would be dealt with severely if I had any more complaints."

"What did I do? Who was it?"

"Missus Arrowood came in here last week and you sold her a set of tires. She claims that you convinced her to get tie rod ends and that she didn't really need tie rod ends. She also says that you overcharged her."

"I...I honestly don't remember that."

Burke bit his bloated bottom lip.

"You don't remember? Good grief, Michael, when are you going to lay off the lightning and get your life in order? Did you sell her tie rod ends without her needing them or not? I mean, we ain't like Hibdons in Norman. We can't just short change customers and expect to stay in business! Do you even understand what the heck I'm saying?"

"But I didn't—"

"Do you want me to call your probation officer and tell them that you aren't doing your job? I'll bet you're hitting the bottle again, huh Michael? No doubt that's why you were late the other day. Sheriff told me that you were passed out over by the playground."

Burke took three steps forward, snatched the broom from Michael's hand and tossed it across the floor of the garage. It landed, ends bouncing, clattering loudly. Burke balled up his fist, extended just his index finger, and proceeded to poke Michael's sternum in a steady pattern.

"I want you to hand over those coveralls and get yourself out of my shop by the end of the day. Clear out your locker, take all your junk, and get the heck out of here."

"But I need this j…"

"What you need is to quit screwing up your life, Michael, and quit screwing everyone else's life up in the process."

Michael took a deep breath. Something rolled around inside his head and then finally found its way out of his mouth.

"Well I don't wanna work for you anyhow, Burke. Every day is just another flippin' insult and a big bitter glass of half empty if you ask me. I am sick of putting up with your loud mouthed garbage and thought about quitting over and over again, but the only thing keeping me here is that I got no place to go."

"Well now you do, Prosper," growled Burke Isaacs, his round face turning bright red. "So I guess you can just get on out of here and go find another job you can get fired from, 'cause I'm done with you."

Burke put his meaty hands on his rotund hips and

curled his lip, not moving, his dark eyes narrowing.

Michael stood still as well, and the two of them like roosters in a hen yard would not budge at all until finally Michael broke the stare and turned toward his locker, his breathing heavy and his chest beginning to swell. He decided not to call Burke on his illogical argument. The guy wanted him gone, so he decided it was best to oblige.

Michael didn't have much in his locker, only a spare set of coveralls, some grease rags, and a package of Saltine crackers. He removed his coveralls and put on his jeans, straightened his sweat dampened t-shirt and after stuffing the coveralls in the locker slammed the rusting grey painted door. Without a word he found his ten-speed, straddled it, and with very little ceremony at all rode out across the Super C Mart parking lot and toward his apartment.

He decided to take the back roads again, zipping through the neighborhoods where the little meager houses lay in perfect rows with little near-perfect yards with people who had good jobs and whose lives weren't screwed up. Tears started welling up in Michael's eyes, blurring the road, and he was thankful that not too many cars took the back roads because he would probably have an accident or something worse.

Even though it was getting hotter it seemed, Michael rode faster to let the wind blow across his body, praying that it would somehow cool him down. The rage inside him, the helpless anger, boiled up

with nowhere to go. Had he truly ruined his life so
badly that this was the best job he could hope to do
for the rest of his life? He struggled so hard to
remember exactly what he had done to deserve such
an existence. His mind couldn't seem to recall the
details, and he knew that people had told him that it
was because he had apparently driven drunk and
hurt someone, but he couldn't remember doing it. He
thought that surely if he had done something so
horrible that he would at least remember some of the
details. Had he burned his brain out on drugs and
alcohol so badly that he could not remember the
cause of his current state?

He turned down another side street and noticed
that all of the houses he passed seemed to be vacant,
no cars parked in the driveways, not a soul to be seen
save a solitary man standing in his yard watering a
patch of brown grass.

Michael stopped his bike on the sidewalk and the
man slouched toward him with his water hose
draining out all over the ground, his coffee cup in his
other hand, a smile forming on his face.

"Can't seem to get this patch to turn green," he
said with a smile that was a little too friendly.

"Are there worms eating it?" asked Michael,
trying to make conversation, his mind still buzzing
from losing his job, breathing in and out heavily from
the bike ride.

The man turned, as if in slow motion, stared at the
patch of brown grass silently, then turned back to face
Michael, that weird smile on his face.

"Don't rightly know," he said, dropping the hose to the ground and pulling up his jogging shorts, wiping his wet hand on his Oklahoma City Thunder t-shirt before thrusting it toward Michael.

"Ross Delbert," he said, that smile maintained. "Don't suppose I know you, young fellah."

Michael hesitated, then put out his hand after wiping some grease on his jeans. They pumped hands for a bit.

"Michael Prosper," he said. "That's what they call me."

Uncomfortable laughter.

Then a long pause as they stared at each other, Ross with the strange smile, his eye twitching oddly, and Michael, on his face something that could only be described as a wince.

"Well," said Delbert scratching his mop of gray hair. "Guess I better get back to it."

The old guy picked up the water hose, water slurrying everywhere, all over the sidewalk, Michael's work boots, the grass, and finally the brown patch.

Silence forced Michael to speak.

"I think if you water it like that you'll drown it," he said, his voice a low stammer. "It's probably cutworms or something. Just need to get some pest..."

Delbert turned on him, his eyes wide, his teeth bared, spittle flying from his mouth.

"Don't you tell me how to take care of my own yard!" he screamed, and sprayed Michael with the water from the hose, its coldness chilling Michael to the bone, and he wouldn't have minded too much if he were a child again playing in the sprinkler, but this was a crazed old guy with some kind of bi-polar disorder.

"Get off my yard!" Ross shouted as he threw the coffee cup, and if Michael didn't duck it would have connected with his right cheek bone rather painfully.

Michael took in a deep breath, his right leg climbing onto his bike, trying to connect with the pedals to get him out of there, to get away from crazed old Mr. Delbert who was obviously mad from yard work, but he just couldn't get his feet to work. Ross was dropping the hose, his fists doubled up, his eyes on fire, one of them filling with blood. He was breathing hard and drool poured from his bottom lip.

"Come here you punk! I'll teach you who to mess with!"

Ross grabbed a handful of Michael's t-shirt before he could fully work the pedals of his bike to roll away from the madman. But then as he was sure he was going to be pummeled by Mr. Delbert, and the bike shifted away with the loosened grasp of the old man on his shirt, Ross Delbert took in a deep breath and started seizing.

Delbert fell to the ground, half on the sidewalk and half on the freshly mowed browning grass and flopped like a late middle aged, human sized fish. Michael stopped, hopped off of his bike, nearly spilling onto the ground himself, and managed to dart over to Ross who convulsed heavily, taking in deep breaths, grunting through clenched teeth, and then froze solid, his arms and legs twisted into a fetal position.

"Oh," Michael said. "Oh man."

He ran across the street, his bike lying discarded on the pavement, and pounded on a door with a nervous fist. In a few moments an old woman came to the door, her hair in curlers, her blue mumu with little flowers scattered all over it, and her sleepy eyes nearly bursting from her face.

"What happened?" she said, her hand producing a cordless phone, one of those old types with the telescoping antenna.

"I don't know," said Michael. "Just started talking and then he went all crazy. No idea."

"Is he dead?" she asked, dialing three numbers on the phone.

"Don't know," he whispered. "I… don't know how to check. Just — afraid to move him."

What happened next was a blur of people, onlookers, paramedics, and finally the sheriff, his white truck pulling up to the scene, emerging with his Silver bottom hat and mirror shades.

Michael made sure he wasn't there to see it.

10: Normalize

From the alarm clock's raucous screeching to the pile of Eggo waffles to the shower and then to the short bus ride, Danny's first day back to school had been a droning blur. When he exited the folding doors of the yellow school bus and set foot just outside the rear entrance to the high school he tried his best to remember what he was supposed to do first. Fortunately for him, someone was there to guide him.

"Woah, Danny," said a petite girl in a royal blue and goldenrod cheer uniform, her auburn hair shining in the morning sun, a glint of silver around her soft neck. "You look like you've been hit by a truck."

She carefully took his hand and then pressed up against him, tiptoeing to kiss his bottom lip, and there was something familiar about it all. He thought about a lab coat —.

"Chemistry," he said plainly, his eyes drifting upward.

She laughed pensively.

"Well, I suppose we have that, you and I…also literally, in five minutes or so."

As this girl guided him to his chemistry class, her green eyes flicking back at him as she walked, his mind was on the three hours his mother had spent at the minor emergency clinic. She did not call, but came back through the door later that night.

"Nothing to worry about," she had said. "He'll be fine."

He had tried to speak to her, but she had gone to her room, "time for bed", and then had turned out the light. He remembered standing at her door for some time, wanting to knock, but listening instead to the eerie silence of the house, their other dog sitting near his feet with the little plastic cone around its neck. He had wandered back to his own room in the same manner that he now wandered into Mr. Dean's chemistry class, and this girl, ah yes, her name is Kallie, Kallie from the picture in his wallet, sat down next to him at the black resin table, pulled out her notebook and pens, produced another notebook and then handed it to him before Mr. Dean started calling roll.

"Good to have you back, Mr. Steren," said a thickly goateed man from the front of the classroom, his eyes regarding him from behind large lensed glasses. "I suppose you will want all of your make-up work right away."

"Y-yes sir," Danny managed. He really didn't want any but knew it was coming.

Class continued, and Danny was faintly aware that Kallie was looking at him now and again with an infectious smile, a look that pulled him in like gravity toward her. Soon he was writing down equations, doing his best to do the math, and since Mr. Dean's classroom was mostly collaborative, Kallie "helped" him with most of it.

Kallie's warm presence comforted him, and she

smelled wonderfully familiar, like vanilla.

When the bell rang Danny approached Mr. Dean to receive his make-up work, a list of assignments the laconic teacher gleefully printed right at his desk, and that was when Danny thought about Grant.

Yes. Grant was in this class.

He turned, seeing Kallie at the door. She checked her small bejeweled watch.

"Mr. Dean," he asked slowly. "Do you think I could get something printed for Arterberry?"

Mr. Dean frowned.

"Arterberry?"

"Yeah," Danny said. "Grant Arterberry. He got bit last night and went to the clinic. Probably sleeping it off."

"Grant...Danny are you ok? I don't know a Grant Arterberry. Never heard of him."

Danny looked over his shoulder again. Kallie pointed at her watch and mouthed "going to be late".

"I...I swear he goes to this class," Danny said. "Are you sure?"

Mr. Dean only shrugged and turned to answer an instant message on his computer, signified by a woman's voice that said "Incoming transmission, Captain."

Danny felt a hand on his arm and it was Kallie, pulling him toward her somewhat sternly.

"Gotta get you to English, hon," she said, her face a worried smile.

Danny felt sick. He did not pull away, however, led along by Kallie as if by the smallest twine as Mr.

Dean spun in his chair to tackle a mound of crookedly stacked papers. The couple filed past students trying to get to their class at the last minute, and Kallie embraced him tightly before whispering in his ear:

"I'll see you at lunch. You have Mr. Bradshaw and then you office aide fourth period. Thought you could use the help today. Don't forget."

Danny was late to English, but Mrs. Parks, a mousy woman with dark hair and a penchant for wearing flowing dresses smiled and excused him as he sat near the front. It wasn't long before other students who apparently were his best friends talked and chatted near him, helping him to find his footing in each of the classes. During most of the conversations he smiled and nodded as if he knew what they were talking about, lost in the fog of his own disordered mind. The next two classes were a blur, with students who seemed to know him very well, joking and laughing around him as he tried to laugh along.

Apparently he was in that crowd referred to by others as "it", a crowd that often let the pain of others be the price for fitting in.

Soon, fourth period arrived and he wandered down the hall, aimlessly looking for some place that he was supposed to go, and a short woman with reddish brown hair popped out of an office and smiled at him.

Donna? Yes, Donna. Admissions secretary.

"Mr. Dean told me about your…well…your confusion in his room. You want to talk about it?"

He paused, took a breath, and nodded.

"I just wanted to get Arterberry's work is all," he said. "Figured I'd help him out."

"Who?"

"Arterberry. Grant Arterberry. He was at my house last night. Got bit by my dog."

Donna put her hands in her pants pockets, looked at the floor, then raised her head to gaze at him, her eyebrows furrowing.

"Danny, this is a small school," she said slowly, as if explaining to a small child. "I have never heard of a student by that name. Are you sure he doesn't go to school at Norman? Do I need to call the school nurse?"

"No," he said, his lips taught. "He came to my house last night and my dog bit him. He texted me for a week while I was in the hospital..."

Danny pulled out his cell phone, pressed the home button and swiped, tapped the green text balloon and scrolled through the names...

Grant wasn't there.

He felt a hand on his shoulder, and turned to see a large man in a shirt and tie.

"You need to check out and go home, Danny?"

"N..No I," and then the room started to spin a bit and he lost his balance for a moment. The large man steadied him by putting his arm around him and taking his hand. Danny shook his head and stood, getting his bearings, looked toward the door and then sat in a nearby chair.

"I'll just sit here if it's ok," he said slowly. "Just

need to think things through."

Donna waved at the large man who exited the office and continued down the hall. Danny thought that it might be Mr. Ellif, the principal, but at the moment faces were somewhat blurred and unnatural, as if his brain had shut off his ability to recognize them.

"You've been through a lot, son," said Donna, and he was thankful he at least knew her name. "If you want we can get Kallie to get your lunch from the cafeteria and bring it down here. That sound ok?"

"Yeah," he said, trying to smile. Kallie's name was the only thing that sounded normal. "That's ok. Thanks."

But it wasn't ok. Nothing was ok. He had sat on his couch last night and talked to Grant Arterberry, had lain in bed last night as all the memories about him started flooding back into his brain, as if the trauma of the dog attack had triggered some kind of memory switch. He'd thought about their trips to the lake to go fishing and swimming in the muddy red-brown waters, the jokes told around camp fires, the plays executed on the football field. He'd even dreamed about some of these memories.

What happened to Grant? Danny didn't care if no one remembered his friend, and he was dead set on figuring out why.

11: Rebuild

The following morning, Michael parked his bike just outside the only other place that seemed halfway familiar: the coffee shop. Upon entering he was immediately greeted by Judith Rigby who, it seemed to him, had not changed her clothing at all. He tried to ignore this.

"Hey, Michael," she said, stuffing a frayed ticket pad in her apron pocket. The stain. The same stain was right there where it had been before.

He nodded involuntarily and followed her to the back where she cleared off a few plates and half empty glasses from a round table then wiped it down with a dingy yellow rag.

"You want me to start with some coffee or would you rather have a soda?" she smiled. "This one ain't on the house."

"Sure, sure, coffee," he said, letting out a deep breath. "I'll take some eggs and link sausage, too... and I'll be sure to pay for it this time. You serve breakfast all day, right?"

"Yeah," she said quickly, but before she could dash off he raised his hand slightly.

"Paper?" he asked.

She looked around, found a newspaper lying on a table, dirty dishes littered around it, folded the paper lengthwise and handed it to him.

"These people ain't using it. S'pose it ain't a problem if you finish it up."

As she began to pour a fresh cup of coffee and then produce a creamer boat and a sugar dispenser, he sat down, opened the paper to the classifieds and started scanning for something that he could do that would pay the bills. He spread the paper out in front of him, turning the thin pages until he found the classifieds section, and started running his finger down the list of jobs, most of them requiring him to use a phone and bother people at dinnertime.

"You know," said Judith who suddenly stood by him. "If you're lookin' for a quick couple of bucks we surely do need a good dish washer. That kid who usually does the job didn't come in again today and Harold is lookin' to replace his sorry behind. We both been bussin' tables and the dishes are stackin' up back there."

"Well, since I don't really have a job, I suppose anything will work at this point. Can't say I ever turned down work."

He had.

"That's a good attitude," she said, her mouth twisting into a smile. "I'll talk to Harold."

She walked through the back door of the dining area which consisted of two old boards hinged on spring swivels like the type one might see on an old west saloon but much more beat up and used. Soon a rather portly balding man emerged wiping his hands on his greasy apron. He removed his hair net and stuffed it into his back pocket, then sat across from Michael and let out a deep sigh.

"So you need some work, Michael?"

Michael's eyes blinked once.

"I don't think I've ever met —"

"— Everyone knows you here, Michael. Small town, remember? Now, am I gonna have any trouble with your…problem?"

"What do you mean?"

Harold smiled the smile of a car salesman.

"I just don't want any trouble. I know you've been in and out of it especially with the accident and all. Lot of folks are not quick to forget what you did. Now I know you served your time, but it takes a while to win back the respect of these townies."

Michael looked at his hands, then at the creamer boat.

"I suppose I do," Michael managed. "But I just need a job. I'll work really hard for you, sir. No trouble, I promise."

"Okay then," said Harold, standing to his feet. "I'll hire you on temporarily. You can start as soon as you finish eating. Don't let me down."

"I won't be any trouble," Michael replied, almost a whisper, watching as Harold moved briskly to the back again and Judith appeared with Michael's meal on a wide plate.

Michael ate his breakfast slowly, wondering what it was that he did that was so bad. He couldn't remember an "accident" and he certainly didn't remember serving time. He wondered when his amnesia would end. He wondered what it would take to try to remember everything or if he really wanted to remember anything. The aching began in his calves again and he reached down to rub one of them. A school bus rolled by the front window along main street, its diesel engine roaring.

By five that afternoon, as he washed the dishes in the back room, the spray nozzle like some kind of strange alien wand, the sour steam rising to swirl around his face, Michael had settled into yet another new job in hopes of piecing together the details of why he was in such a state, until he looked up and saw someone strangely familiar.

Who is that?

He stared, his face a blank mask of confusion, looking through the small service window that faced out into the restaurant just past Howard who grilled a quad of hamburger patties. Michael's mind began to clear as he stared blankly, his hands holding a sudsy dish and a sponge. Sitting at a table near the middle of the dining area, talking to a dark-headed teenage boy was Kalila Steren, the girl who went to prom with him, the girl who was always on his arm in high school, the girl he had wronged so deeply that night who then moved away to find someone else, someone in the military.

Just then she looked in his direction and by reflex he looked away, but it was only a casual glance and she didn't notice him. He looked at her again, but this time she was laughing and lightly punching the teen on the shoulder, then tousling his hair.

When did she get into town? Oh Kalila…I'm so sorry…

And then the guilt washed over him as he

dropped the plate and the sponge into the soapy water. What he did, and then what she did, flooded back to his mind in vivid detail which caused him to pull the heavy yellow rubber gloves off of his hands and walk to the back of the restaurant to exit out the back door. The sudden urge to drink seized his bones and made them ache. He felt around in his pockets for a cigarette and then couldn't remember if he smoked or not, and when he didn't find anything he thought maybe that he didn't. He stood in the alley leaning against the outside wall, feeling the rough brick rake against his back through his thin shirt. After a moment of this, Judith popped out, her eyebrows furrowed.

"Don't make a fool of me Michael," she said, trying to keep her tone light. "Now get your butt back in there and get to work."

Tears began to well up in Michael's eyes and he rubbed them out with the back of his hand.

"I just don't think I can face some of the people of my past, Judith," he slurred. "I think I've done some very bad things and I just don't know how to get past it all. I...I sometimes don't remember what I did and I'm not even sure I think I did it, but everyone seems to think I did —"

"Michael," and her hand was on his arm, gently yet firmly. "You have to get back in there. We can talk about it after work if you want. Go to Sonic and get a shake or something. Right now we need to get back to the job."

She paused, rubbed his shoulder.

"I know you've been through a lot, Michael, but people can be forgiving if you let them. You just have to take it one day at a time. All of us do things we regret, but we can't let those things control us. We have to find grace somewhere. That grace is good when you find it, and maybe your time is comin'."

This seemed to sate him, and he nodded quietly and then walked past her through the door and into the restaurant again. Soon he was back to washing dishes as if he were a robot programmed to do the task, his face sullen and drawn, an automatic man, staring down at the soapy water, his eyes never rising to look out the service window. After a bit, his sorrow subsided, and he was able to finish his shift without much more trouble.

He would have to rebuild what he thought his life might be, for he felt that whatever had happened to him to make him forget his transgression was lingering in the fringes of the world, its devastating effect on others something that they could not forget even if he could not remember. He hoped normalcy would return to him, and he hoped that it contained something for which he could forgive himself.

He decided to work until closing as he poured himself into a few more hours of manual labor, and he found that he had spent the entire day without eating, only stopping to take a sip from a glass of ice water that Judith had brought to him. Before he could realize how late it had become, Harold was locking the front door and turning out the lights.

"Time to go home, punkin'," said Judith hanging

her apron on a peg in the back room and then emerging to slap him on the shoulder. "Wanna take me up on that shake?"

A shake sounded good.

12: Redacted

Baseball practice was a drag for him.

Danny sat in the dugout, a big bucket of David's sunflower seeds near his left foot, dressed out but not playing. Since he had been sidelined for his concussion, Coach Wood didn't feel it was appropriate to let him do anything at all save sit still and watch the other players have a good time.

Sitting beside him, her black frame glasses a little cockeyed, her sandy blond hair in a pony tail, Amanda Abrams cracked another sunflower seed with her teeth.

"Don't worry about it, Danny," she said. "You'll be back out there playing again before you know it."

Danny only nodded, his mind spinning back toward the odd forgetfulness of seemingly everyone he knew, and the fact that everyone around him had forgotten that Grant Arterberry existed. The looks on their faces caused him not to push it. Caused him to recoil from asking any more questions. The worst thing, the thing that made him sick, that caused him to think that he was losing his mind, was when he called home to talk to his mother.

The phone rang a few times and then went to voicemail. He called again. This time she picked up, and he heard her voice shrouded in background noise that sounded like someone reading off a string of numbers.

"Hey mom," he said. "How'z it going?"

"Fine, son," she replied. "Is everything all right?"

"Yeah, I guess. Um...How is Grant doing? Have you talked to him this morning?"

There was a pause on the phone, and he could hear the voice, the voice speaking a random string of numbers...4..2..4..6..8..1...

"Grant?" she said methodically, tonelessly. "I... I'm not sure what you mean. Are you ok?"

"Mom. Grant Arterberry came by last night to visit. He stopped in, we had a few laughs, and then our dog bit him. The Shih Tzu."

"Danny we only have one dog and it's not a Shih Tzu. Maybe you need to come home and rest."

Not one thing about Grant. She wouldn't even say his name. Danny had then changed the subject and this had seemed to calm his mother a bit.

But now Danny sat and watched his teammates toss the ball around the field, listening to the baseball slap leather gloves at high velocities, and he wondered if he was losing his mind.

"You get all your makeup work, Danny?" asked Amanda spitting out a sunflower seed shell onto the sandy dirt. "You need any help with any subject, I'm your girl."

She winked at him.

He tried not to crack a smile but couldn't help it. She was sort of pretty behind those thick glasses he supposed, and her teeth were very white, like she bleached them. She nudged him with her elbow.

"I suppose I got it all," he offered, but she continued as if she had rehearsed this conversation already.

"Really, man," she half laughed. "I'm a straight 'A' student. School's easy for me. Gotta keep you eligible so that when you do feel like playing again you'll be ready for anything."

"Hey Abrams!" yelled Coach Wood wiping a rag across his forehead. "Get the water out!"

She laughed nervously and patted Danny on the shoulder before running over to grab the water bottles in her little basket and then jogging out to the players who all began to gather around her, each of them taking long swigs, their fitted caps coming off, some of them using them as fans.

Coach Wood jogged over to the dugout, grunted through the gate and sat his bulk down beside Danny on the bench. The bench creaked beneath him, and then Danny felt Coach Wood's heavy arm around his shoulder.

"It's gonna be ok, Danny," he said, his voice loud in Danny's ear. "You'll be back on top really soon. Just gotta get you healed up is all."

Danny didn't say anything. Didn't want to talk about Grant. Didn't want to rock the boat. Coach Wood leaned back against the wall, straightened out his leg and reached in his pocket then handed Danny a small pill bottle.

"I want you to take this co-enzyme q10," he said. "At least until you can play again. Make sure you take it before your workout and then stay in the gym. I suspect you'll be back on the field in a few weeks, and probably if you're lucky...and *we're* lucky...

won't miss the playoffs. That a deal?"

"Yeah, Coach," said Danny, his face sullen. "I guess so. Thanks."

"Allright, Danny. Suck it up, ok? You're makin' us all feel bad. Not a good thing going up against Lexington tonight. Now get to the gym."

The heavy arm lifted, but then Coach slapped him on the back. It stung. Danny chuckled a bit as he watched Coach jog carefully back out to the field and order out some batting practice.

After a short walk through the football field, Danny found himself at the main athletic building. The metal door, propped open with a wooden wedge, revealed a room full of workout equipment and a few fans that sat on the floor cranked to full blast. The radio sat on a shelf to his left, screamo metal blaring, and a few students were using the free weights. As ordered, he popped open the supplement bottle and swallowed one of the pills dry. Already dressed out in shorts and a tee shirt, he started stretching his legs.

"Hey cutie," came a familiar voice.

He spun around. There in the door stood Kallie Norris, her finger twirling a strand of her red-brown hair.

"Kallie I don't think you are supposed to be here right now," he said. "Like, regulations or something."

"Yeah, like that ever stopped me," she giggled. "I promise I'll stand at the door and won't come in."

He walked calmly over to her, and then was going to ask her something about someone. Couldn't remember his name...or was it a her? Arter...

something. Not really sure. She took his hand and leaned in to plant her lips on his, and he didn't respond. She pulled back, smiled widely and then rolled her eyes, the familiar rolling of the eyes, up and to the left.

"You ok, sweetheart?" she asked, and he could smell her perfume, a sweet lingering vanilla.

"Yeah," he stammered. "I...I think so."

"I'll go," she said. "I think you'll be ok without me. Besides, if you don't get busy with your workout Coach Wood will have a serious meltdown."

She left him, and as he started into his workout his mind began to relax, to fall into the sweet embrace of normalcy, of routine, of the welcome and familiar methodical rhythms of lifting weights, of the machines. Later, when his mother came to pick him up from school, she asked him about his academic workload, about Kallie, and when they went to the cafe to eat dinner that night he found himself joking with his mother about their sole dog Bella and how she would have to get the restraint cone removed soon so that she would quit banging into the furniture.

Neither of them noticed the longing looks of the man washing dishes in the kitchen.

13: Abend

Saturday shift. It would be an all day affair.

Michael was grateful for the hours he would work. Burke never let him work so many hours, and Howard seemed to be a better boss, went to a church somewhere in town that Michael had been to as a teen but never went back.

Michael grabbed an apron, Judith greeting him with a smile, as they stood around the first hour before they opened, the smell of fresh biscuits baking in the ovens. Harold had been here much earlier, making them from scratch.

"You get much sleep, Michael?" said Judith, trying to make conversation.

"Not really," he replied. "Just tossed and turned. It's been a weird couple of days what with the memory loss, but I'm starting to come back to myself."

"What happened to cause that memory loss, son?" asked Harold, peeking into the oven to check the biscuits.

"Don't really know," said Michael, his eyes scanning the floor. "I just woke up near that playground over on fifth and don't really remember how I got there."

"Could be a blackout," offered Judith. "My cousin was a...well...an addict, too, and he'd have blackouts even after he'd been clean and sober for a while. Maybe that's it."

They all stood around for a second, the uncomfortable silence thick in the air, until Michael let them off easy.

"Yeah," he said, cracking a cautious smile. "I guess when you pound back the brew like I used to then you bound to break something in the process."

The three of them chuckled, Judith a little too loud, and Michael could tell that he had eased their tension a bit.

After a short breakfast, Michael cleaned their dishes and then Harold opened the doors for two old men wearing ball caps, the cheap kind with the plastic snap strip in back. They nodded at Judith, men of few words who had come to drink coffee and read the paper.

The day dragged on, and after the lunch rush Michael had just finished drying all the plates and had put them away when he saw a flash of red which staggered him a bit, and then his head began to pound as if someone had hit him from behind.

He cried out.

"You ok, Michael?" asked Judith looking through the service window past the warmers.

Michael didn't answer for a second, and then Judith was by his elbow, helping him over to a table near the kitchen entrance where she began fanning him with her apron.

"He ok?" asked Harold, wiping his hands on a rag. "I'll get him some water."

"No, no, I'm fine," slurred Michael. "I just need to rest a bit. Probably all that steam back there. A little light-headed."

Harold and Judith were soon sitting on either side of him at the table, but not for long. A few late lunch patrons shuffled in the door and the two darted away to serve them, Judith looking pensively back at Michael as he sat tracing one square on the checkered table cloth with his index finger.

"This seat taken, Mikey old boy?" asked a familiar voice, cold and gravelly.

Sheriff Norris stood across the table from Michael, his Stetson in his hand, aviators in his shirt pocket near his shiny badge, the teeth in his crooked grin forming a shark-like smile.

"No," Michael offered. "Not really."

The sheriff pulled out a chair, its legs groaning across the floor, and then Michael heard the chair creak as the sheriff's bulk fell upon it.

"Looks like you got yourself another job. That's good. What happened over at the Sinclair?"

"Nothing. Just a difference of opinion. I tried to help a lady and she complained is all. Burke and I got in an argument and then he fired me. Plain and simple."

"Plain and simple," he smiled again. "Judith!"

She scurried over to him, ticket pad in hand.

"I'll have the usual," he said. "Slide some bacon on it this time, though."

"Coming right up," she said, her face blank, as if the sheriff had something on her.

She's afraid of him, too.

They both sat in silence for a bit.

"Now," grunted the sheriff. "You clean and sober or did you hit a little before coming to work?"

"I'm clean and sober, sheriff," Michael said, his lips tightening a bit, his eyes wide. "I ain't touched a drop since at least when we talked the other day after I woke up. I'd appreciate it if you would stop harassing me about it."

Norris put up his hands, palms toward Michael, that grin returning.

"I'm just here for your welfare, Michael, that's all. I don't want any trouble."

A plate with a load of steak fries and a sandwich with what looked like breaded chicken and bacon on it slid in front of him.

"Thank's, darlin'," said the sheriff, but Judith's smile was strained, not like it usually was with customers.

Michael shot a glance toward the kitchen but could not see Howard anywhere. He thought about Ross Delbert, the man who greeted him over on fifth before spraying him with water and then falling into a seizure. He thought about telling the sheriff, but then he had fled the scene. He just wanted to know. He had to know.

"I...I don't know how to say this, and I don't want you to blame me..."

The sheriff looked up from his meal, holding the sandwich in his thick hands, his eyes staring as if looking through Michael with x-ray vision.

"What'd you do?"

"Nothing, really, honest. I just...I saw something

79

the other day and wondered..."

"Wondered what? Spit it out."

"Ok," he said, starting to ball up a napkin in his hands. "I was riding back after getting fired earlier this week and I rode down fifth street and there was Ross Delbert watering his lawn. Guy just started talking to me, then he went all ballistic and then he had like a seizure or something, then he fell down. I called for help, but didn't stay...too much trouble. Ambulance was there. Did you work that? I mean, how is he doing? You heard anything?"

"Can't say that I do," said the sheriff, taking a huge bite of his sandwich, then turning toward the kitchen, mouth full. "Great job, Howard. Lifelike representation. Just like mom used to make."

"But..." Michael continued. "Ross Delbert...what happened to him? Really, sheriff. I need to know."

Norris shot a hand out and grabbed Michael by the wrist, shaking the table so that the silverware rattled, his face becoming stone, a small dollop of mayonnaise on his iron chin.

"Don't know anything about it, Mikey," he grunted. "Just an ordinary day in Noble."

"Excuse me," Michael whispered, pulling away from the sheriff who released him from the vice grip that was his beefy hand. "I'll just finish my break outside."

The sheriff only laughed as Michael walked to the front of the cafe, exited the doors and stood on the sidewalk, then leaned against the brick wall between the door and the pane glass window. He closed his eyes, thinking about Ross Delbert, wondering why the sheriff did not remember him, why he was so flippant about it, and when he opened his eyes he began looking toward the blue sky, not a cloud to be seen, only a haze far off.

He noticed something else, though, something strange. In the distance, just within the range of his vision, rising above the row of houses at the edge of town, he could see the long thin wisp of what could only be a dust devil, its swirling motion unmistakable, but completely foreign to this part of the country.

A noise came from inside, a child crying, and he turned to look through the plate glass window, but something a reflection in the glass made him turn around and look across the street. When he refocused his vision he was staring at the vagrant who had stood outside his window, and their eyes met.

Michael crossed the street, looking briefly for cars, but easily navigating to the other side. The homeless man stood quietly, yet he shuffled from foot to foot, his hands wringing, his bloodshot eyes darting nervously, and Michael thought that he might run away if he came close, but the old guy stood his ground. When Michael stepped up onto the curb, the man shot out a hand, palm facing out toward him like some bizarre crossing guard. The bloodshot eyes popped open wide and a wheezy groan escaped his cracked lips.

"Stop right there," stammered the old man.

"What do you want from me?" asked Michael, his

teeth grinding. "I don't like being stalked."

"I'm not trying to scare you. I'm just trying to wake you up."

Michael put his hands on his hips.

"Look, bud. I don't really know what you mean by that, and I'm sure you have some reason why you —"

"Go see for yourself!" the vagrant shouted, his dirt-blackened bony finger pointing down the street. "You go see for yourself and you'll see the nothing, the nothing that's wrong! Help us both. Go see it."

Michael suddenly felt something flip inside his stomach, something squirming in there that wanted to escape from his mouth, and he staggered back and placed his hand on a nearby lamppost for support. His eyes closed tight, little red stars dancing in the blackness, and when he opened them the homeless man was shambling up the sidewalk, placing his grubby hand on the walls of the shopfronts for stability, as if he were suffering from the same symptoms.

Michael followed, his stomach beginning to normalize, his breathing becoming more even, but the homeless man disappeared around a corner just as Michael heard someone shouting at him. He spun around to see Harold in the distance, his face red, his eyes very visible from this distance.

"Michael!" he screamed. "What are you doing!? We need you back here!"

Slowly, his face drawn, Michael turned his feet and jogged back across the street to find his way back to the front door of the cafe, passing by a wheezing Harold. Michael scraped his feet on the carpet as he resumed his post, but deep in his mind the strangeness of the meeting with the homeless man would not leave him and sat vulture-like in the recesses of his brain.

The sheriff did not leave a tip.

14: Script

"Son," came the gentle voice of his mother accompanied with a gentle jab to the ribs. "Get up or we'll be late for church."

"Church?" he intoned involuntarily.

"Yes," she said, a towel wrapped around her head, toothbrush in hand, visible just over the edge of his comforter. "Now get out of bed before I drag you out."

When she stomped out of the room, Danny thought about the night before, the three hours spent at Pizza Hut with friends, faces that had somehow become more and more familiar and welcoming, the odd jokes using internet memes as punchlines, the sheer normalcy of it all. He had dragged in at nearly three a.m, no alcohol imbibed (at least by him) and a warm kiss at his doorstep given to him by Kallie Norris.

He had closed his eyes.

Another scream from his mother and he stumbled out of bed, filed into the shower, found a nice Tony Hawk shirt and some slightly ripped jeans and slipped on his green Chuck Taylors before downing a glass of milk and an Oreo flavored pop tart.

Breakfast of champions.

He shut the door behind him because his mother was waiting in her little red car, her phone out not to call someone or to text, but to check the time that was slipping ever so quickly away. Her eyes were furrowed and her mouth drawn thin.

The ride to church did not include conversation, only the common road noise and that annoying radio station his mother always tuned to just before going to church, the station not listened to during the week, only on Sunday morning. All he could think about at the moment was that he would be soon playing baseball with his friends.

They arrived a little too late for Sunday school and after shuffling through the doors he found Kallie waiting on him, her large father standing a few feet away, and Danny watched his strangely jovial expression melt away to reveal something much more cold, like something from one of those old westerns where the hero has just strutted through the saloon doors and the local gang gives him the stink eye.

Kallie's face however, a near perfect copy of his mother's yet without all the laugh lines, lit up with wide green eyes. She bounced over to him to take his hand, the silver locket around her neck reflecting the overhead lamps.

"Wanna sit with us?" she asked, a little giggle escaping her lips.

"Um, no," he said. "I don't think your dad would approve."

She looked back at the sheriff who tried to change his scowl to a half-smile, but couldn't quite manage it.

"Oh he won't bite," she laughed. "Just don't talk to him directly. I'll sit between the two of you."

Danny looked at his mother, a smirk floating across her gaze before she gave him a toothy smile.

"I'm not sitting by myself, if that's what you're asking," said Kalila

"Oh, no, Mrs. Steren," said Kallie. "I insist that you sit with us, too."

Kallie took Danny's hand as if things were settled even though the expression on Danny's face could be read by all as fear mixed with uncertainty. Danny walked through the foyer and Kalila followed as if she were his helpless satellite. Soon all of them stood just outside the main entrance to the sanctuary, an uncomfortable silence hanging thick in the air.

Kallie sliced through it.

"Let's sit somewhere different this time," she said, seemingly unfazed by her father's wordless gaze at Danny.

Danny thought that the old sheriff looked kind of strange without his uniform, standing there in that suit and tie he looked like a big mafia don, his dark hair slicked back with what could only be hair oil, parted on one side, his head a chiseled granite bust rising out of his freshly pressed collar. He lazily wondered what it must be like to find clothing for such a massive man.

Linebackers 'R' Us.

They found their seat, but Danny's mother ended up sitting next to Sheriff Norris because the aisles became crowded and she misstepped. Just as Kallie had promised she became a conflict barrier between Danny and her father. Danny took in a deep breath and let it out as they sat down, and suddenly the familiarity of his environment faded away until he couldn't really remember ever going to church before. Strangely, the act of going to church seemed familiar, but the sanctuary with its high stained glass windows, its fine wood interior, felt weird and out of place.

Far to the front of the room stood a large stage where there were several people sitting in rows of chairs, all of them wearing purple robes with white sashes. Some men sat on smaller benches in front of them but these men all wore dark suits with dark ties. A large polished wooden lectern rose out of the middle of the stage in the shape of a giant cross, and an older man, his gray ring of hair around a bald spot, tapped the microphone once before asking everyone to stand.

The singing began, an inharmonious chorus, and the words posted on huge screens on either side of the stage told the tale of rote lyrics, wispy colored backgrounds animated behind them, swirling and spinning, and it seemed to Danny that the colors somehow made him feel less uncomfortable even though he was an arm's length away from Kallie's golem-like father. Danny didn't know the words, but he tried to sing them, follow along. He looked around at the faces of all of the people, but their expressions were not readable, each of them focused on the swirling colors, each of them a blank mask.

The people sat and stood on commands given by the man at the podium, none of them chatting with each other, only listening for the next order, and Danny began to feel more and more uncomfortable.

He watched as another man approached the podium
with a book, and when he opened it the people all
opened their own, but he did not have a book. He
knew that it was the Bible, but it didn't look right,
and he couldn't make out the words on the pages of
Kallie's. A prim lady next to him muttered "amen"
once in a while to punctuate the speech of the man at
the podium who read verses from his book
punctuated by strings of numbers, numbers which
were mumbled by the prim lady and by Kallie,
whispered so that they were nearly inaudible. He
tried to read the words on the page in Kallie's book
but he couldn't see them clearly, as if they were blurry
and he needed glasses to read them, and he tried to
get Kallie's attention but she was focused on what the
man was saying as he led everyone in prayers,
listening for the cues from the audience that consisted
of "amen", "yes", and "preach it".

Danny could not focus on what the man was
saying, a huge headache forming, but mostly his
speech had to do with finding a purpose for one's life,
for gaining acceptance of others, and of general things
to make one feel pretty good. Danny did not feel
pretty good, and as a matter of fact he was beginning
to feel more and more out of place. The robotic eyes
of the crowd around him, his girlfriend included, and
his own mother seemed distant, drawn, and
absolutely inhuman.

All but the sheriff, who caught Danny's gaze once
which made Danny look at his lap.

Without much ceremony, the services ended, and

they were headed out the door to the car again, Kallie giving him a kiss on the cheek, looking back at her father who had resumed practising his scowl, and once Danny had entered the car and they were on their way home he decided to say something to his mother about it.

"What was the deal with church?" he asked.

"What do you mean?"

"Is that how church is supposed to be? All plotted out like a machine?"

She reached over and placed her right hand on his wrist.

"Oh honey," she said. "Church is over. We don't have to talk about it anymore."

His eyebrows furrowed.

"I...seem to remember us being much more involved in church. What happened?"

"Well," she laughed. "I guess that's just in the past. C'mon! We've been to church. Done our duty. Now we go eat. Where you wanna go?"

He sat in silence for a moment, his mind trying to remember a church camp moment or something that sat on the edge of his ability to recall it.

"How about Kendall's?" she said, her eyes widening. "Ice cream for dessert."

"Yeah, I guess."

He looked out the window as they drove by the church, watching the people file out into the parking lot and into their cars like ants moving to their respective jobs and wondered what he was trying so hard to remember.

15: Refactor

Michael sat on a concrete parking stop in the front lot of his apartment complex, an IBC root beer in hand, wishing it was made of hops and barley rather than root.

It was a clear Sunday night and the stars, like small bits of glitter on a black velvet backdrop, winked on and off independently, the moon a fat blob that shed a bluish light on everything, the color washing the world in a hue that matched Michael's mood.

He had been sitting on this parking stop for quite some time, the tears now completely dry on his cheeks yet the residue making his skin feel tight. He thought about Kalila wandering into the cafe again that day with her son in tow. He was a tall young man with dark hair and a rather dazed look about him.

They had ordered hamburgers and had ice cream for dessert, and he had stood in the back washing dishes, wondering if he could ever have the nerve to go out and talk to her. Why would he? It had been years since they knew each other, years since the awkward silences that dominated their meetings after their one night stand. He had embarrassed her, the daughter of a prominent figure in this town. She had returned to Noble for some reason, a reason that he couldn't understand, especially after what he had done.

"Michael," Howard had said, shaking him out of his trance. "Get out there and bus a few tables, would you? Judith is going on break while it's died down out there."

"Sure thing," he had replied, almost mechanically.

He had known that he would have to go out there, hope she didn't recognize him, had wondered how she would react.

Stepping through the swinging doors to the dining area he had pushed a resin cart that carried a pan with soapy water and a rag. He had begun clearing dishes from the first table and wiping it down, and then glanced over to see Kalila staring at him. He had cracked a nervous smile, at which she had looked back down at her half empty bowl of ice cream. Her son had been talking to her about something, and he had noticed her facial expression so he had turned around to see who she had seen.

Michael had seen his own face.

The young man was a younger version of him, and that suspicion had risen within him, producing a truth. The boy was his. There was no mistaking it. Same eyes, hair, cheek bones, even the way the puffy area just above his eyes hung down slightly to look like he was squinting.

Michael had dropped a plastic plate on the floor and it had clattered, and then Kalila and her son had risen. She had snatched the check as they had walked to the front of the cafe where Harold stood, looking at Michael with his eyebrows furrowed, but then turning to smile at Kalila who suddenly looked as if she had seen a dead man rise from the grave. The young man had been completely non-plussed, pulling out his smart phone to text someone.

Michael had bent down, cleaning up the mess he had made, and then the rest of the day he had worked through his shift, trying his best to hold in his emotion, the hurt building up in his chest to eventually avalanche out of him this evening as he sat down on the parking stop to cry and cry.

He stood slowly, shuffling his feet to a broken down set of outdoor furniture that had been placed there at one time in hopes of beautifying an already run down and paint-chipped facade. It creaked beneath his weight as he sat down, and he set his near empty bottle of IBC on the uneven table to then place his hand across his eyes and wiped them, finishing by rubbing the bridge of his nose.

If only things were different. The prom night that went so wrong, the sadness and eventual shock of her leaving town, the inevitable news that she had married a military man, the guilt of her giving herself to him out of fear that it would not be acceptable to their "friends" if their prom night had not gone any other way. So young and so unaware of the truth of life.

He supposed that if he were to spend his current days thinking about the "if only's" of his life then there would be no moving forward. But what about this current life of his was indeed "moving forward" at all? He could not think of anything about his current situation that would qualify as a "forward moving life."

He did the only thing that came natural to him, tilting his head back and staring at the stars, and that was when he noticed the strangeness of the sky, the odd greenish ribbon that had begun to form there, and thought that an aurora borealis would be a most uncommon display for an Oklahoma sky.

But what was it?

The ribbon grew in size, the middle filling with a glorious lemon yellow that glowed and blended with the kelly green outer edges, until the center shifted to a white hot core that snaked throughout, the waves eddying out from it in motions that seemed to him to need to make sounds, but it was indeed silent. It waved in the sky as if it were a long flowing standard on the end of an invisible pole, stretching out across the black, star dotted sky like a luminous snake seen only around the fourth of July. It stretched toward the moon, waving left and right, wriggling like a glow worm, its function unknown to him.

And then he got a really good look at the moon, and noticed that it, too, did not look right. Something about the way that its craters did not form the perceived man who had for centuries, millennia, stared down at humans who had made a cognitive choice to see the pattern. No. This was not a face at all. This was some type of strange, nondescript design, craters that formed something unknown to him. And as soon as it had appeared, the ribbon had vanished, as if someone had wiped it from the sky like a smudge on a screen.

No noise. No flashes. Only the soft spring breeze that seemed to be much too hot for this time of year. In that breeze, strangely, there was a grit that got in between Michael's teeth, the grit that only comes from a long stretch of desert dunes and hopeless wasteland.

16: Upgrade

"Ok everyone, let's go to the computer lab."

Danny shuffled out the door with the rest of his class, all of them abuzz not about the end of instruction testing that was about to inevitably control their lives, but about whatever most teens talk about when they get perceived free time.

Kallie only wanted to talk to him about the weekend.

"So what do we have planned this Saturday?" she asked, that grin as if to say she knew what he was thinking.

She didn't.

"I...I don't know, Kallie. It's only Monday. Haven't thought that far ahead," Danny whispered, noticing Mr. DeFord walking right behind him, his large glasses being pushed up on his nose by one finger.

DeFord smiled.

"I guess we could go to the Warren in Moore," Danny said, turning back around and taking her hand. "I haven't been there in a while and I'd like to see something in IMAX."

"Those things give me a headache," she said, squeezing his hand. "What about just...well...we can talk about it later."

They all rounded the corner and proceeded up the hallway to the computer lab which was a former typing classroom that had been filled with older

Pentium 4 computers.

"Each of you find a computer and log in," said Mr. DeFord sitting down at the lead computer at the front of the room. It had two screens linked together so that he could move things around and use the nanny program that monitored what all students were seeing on their computer screens.

"Everyone sit at your designated seat number. I have ordered them accordingly so that you will not be sitting next to your usual friends."

Groans.

"I know, I know," said Mr. DeFord, smiling apologetically and raising his hands, palms out. "It's just so you will not be distracted and so you will do your best."

"Um, Mr. DeFord," said Tommy Nolan, his platinum blonde hair cut in a perfectly square flat-top. "This is just a practice test, right?"

"It is for a very real grade, Tommy," said Mr. DeFord, his dark eyebrows furrowing. "Just do your best."

Kallie brushed Danny's hand with hers and Danny caught her eye as she went to her assigned seat before he methodically found his own at the far front right corner of the room near the window, the one nearest Mr. DeFord.

After everyone had logged in (even Danny Rolston who seemed to have been born in a time deep in the past before they invented torches), Mr. DeFord directed them to the online U.S. History practice test and soon all of the students were quietly settling in for a class period of clicking, typing and submitting answers. Soon Danny's head began to throb a bit from eye strain, and he rubbed his temple with his thumb and index finger. He took a deep breath and then exhaled slowly as he answered question after question, not taking advantage of the handy highlighting or elimination tools provided to him on his smallish flat screen.

Twenty five questions later he had submitted his test to the automatic scorer, balked at his mediocre score, thought about the insanity of not including anything about the Civil War on a U.S. History test, and clicked away to open up a browser window in search of random humor and rage comics, some of which were not blocked by the net-nanny server the school used.

He heard a growl, realizing that it was only Mr. DeFord clearing his throat as he graded paper after paper with his signature purple pen. DeFord looked up briefly to make eye contact with Danny and then went right back to work.

Danny Googled theater showtimes at the Warren.

He found several listings for the Warren theater, clicked on the top link and then waited for the server to update his page and take him to the movie listings.

He waited.

The screen went white for a moment and then after a moment turned blue and a message appeared:

Internal Server Error
The server encountered an internal error or due to

misconfiguration was unable to complete your request. Please contact the system administrator for further assistance.

He stared at the screen for a moment before clicking the back button on the browser only to find that he had been returned to the main Google search screen. He raised his hand.

"What do you need, Danny?" asked Mr. DeFord evenly.

"I think my computer has a glitch or something."

"Tell me what's new."

They both grinned knowingly and Danny went back to searching Google, but each time he clicked on something in the list of links the screen displayed the "internal server error" message again and then Danny would click the back button until he returned to the Google start page.

Then he noticed something at the top right of the screen, something blue and blinking, just a small blue block of pixels that blinked on and off faintly, and when he clicked it, the screen began to dance with color and the Google logo melted away to reveal a full screen of scrolling symbols of a type unfamiliar to him. It did not look like the Wingdings font or any other strange symbol pattern, but was full of concentric circles, strange dodecahedrons, red-orange blobs of uneven marks resembling the spattering of some type of fluid on the screen.

And then Mr. DeFord fell to the floor, writhing around uncontrollably, his black fright wig hair wiggling, his glasses falling to the worn blue-green carpet. Danny stood to his feet, knocking his chair back behind him, but before he could help his teacher, DeFord stood to his feet as if nothing happened, wiped his mouth with the back of one heavy hand and walked to the door of the computer lab, eyes darting around nervously while every student but Danny worked away as if they had not seen their teacher become momentarily helpless on the floor. Mr. DeFord exited the room, his head jerking back and forth involuntarily.

Without prompting Danny followed, and as he stepped out into the hallway in pursuit of Mr. DeFord, he watched as his teacher slipped quietly through the doorless entry way of the boy's bathroom just down the hall. Danny pursued at a safe distance, knowing that being in the hallway without a pass would bring detention, but he was concerned about Mr. DeFord. Danny stopped, hesitated, then moved back to the safety of the classroom threshold.

"Mr. DeFord, are you alright?" he called, his hand resting on the wall next to him.

He looked back through the open door into the classroom. His classmates, Kallie, all typing away on their keyboards, clicking their cursors on answers, completely lost in thought, were somehow oblivious to the scene that played out in front of them.

Reconsidering, he moved down the vacant hall, the incandescent lights washing it in an eerie glow, and peered into the bathroom.

"Mr. DeFord?" he called.

No answer.

He went in, turned the corner of the short hall that shielded the bathroom from being open to the main hall, and stood in the small bathroom, no sign of Mr. DeFord. He walked further, checking the three toilet stalls, finding no one, hearing his own footfalls echo strangely on the hard tile floor.

But he went in here. Where did he go?

Backing up, he slowly returned to the classroom, his face stretched in a grimace, and when he entered the classroom again his mouth dropped open involuntarily.

Sitting at the main computer station, Mr. DeFord sat grading papers.

He looked up from his papers, his signature glasses not on his face, a purple grading pen in hand which he now used to grip as if it were a small baton.

"Danny," he said, his voice stern, gravelly. "Why did you leave the classroom without permission?"

Danny opened his mouth to speak, but Mr. DeFord, at least who Danny thought might be Mr. DeFord, cut him off.

"No need to explain, sir. Just report to after school detention. This is a state test, after all. I know it is a practice test, but you could at least take it seriously."

Danny thought about speaking, but his mouth pressed itself into a frown, his eyes squinted tight, and he crossed the room to his assigned seat to wait out the rest of the class period. He looked across at Kallie, but her eyes stared deeply into the screen in front of her as if she were mesmerized, her pretty green eyes dancing as she focused on the practice test.

Danny stewed for a moment, wondering whether he had blacked out again, wondering if his headache was any indication of his sudden lapse in memory. He swore that Mr. DeFord fell on the floor and seized. He clearly remembered it, but then he watched as Mr. DeFord reached down, picked up his glasses from where he left them on the floor, put them on and then pushed them onto his nose with one steady finger.

That was when Danny knew he wasn't crazy, but something deep inside his soul quivered.

17: Control

The old high school looked the same to him.

Some fresh paint, a new press box on the football field, a couple of portable buildings to house the growing number of students. Noble had apparently rezoned its district.

Michael had been out for an early afternoon bike ride since the cafe closed up on Mondays to give the staff time off from working all weekend. He had ridden nearly every main street since he woke up late that morning. He found it very relaxing after all the strangeness that had occurred over the past few days. Things were becoming more normal again, but the nagging feeling that events could suddenly change for the worse would not leave him.

He had come to rest just across the street from the football field, a desperate attempt to relive his glory days that had just this morning come flooding back to his memory. The field house sat on the other end, an ultramodern white building with a strange industrial look, nowhere close to the old barn that used to be there when he wore pads and a helmet. Beyond the field house high on a hill sat the high school, and as he watched, the distant echo of the school bell sounding across the freshly mowed grass and several students began to exit the main building.

From this distance he couldn't make out any faces, but from the way the boy walked he recognized a familiar gait. It was Kalila's son, the boy in the cafe from whom he had averted his gaze. This time he did not turn away, but strained his eyes to see, squinting, and noticed that the boy was striding to the field house in a fit of rage.

Something was wrong.

He couldn't say how he knew this. He simply knew. It was instinctual, something that went without saying, a body language that seemed very easy to understand.

It was his body language.

As the boy disappeared into the side door of the field house, Michael climbed onto his bike and with some effort pedaled away, on down forty-eighth street, passing by the Pentecostal Holiness church, down a side street and then back toward his apartment complex. As he rode, his eyes began to water, not with the wind blowing in his face, but with the overwhelming sadness that welled up in him and overflowed from his heart. It poured from him, his chest beginning to hitch uncontrollably until he stopped near a driveway and leaned on a brick enclosed mailbox to gain some semblance of control.

He stood silently, his nose running a bit, and when he raised his head to wipe his forearm across his mouth, he noticed an elderly woman in a pink nightgown standing inside her front door just inside a glass outer door, a flyswatter in one hand and a cordless phone in the other. He waved nervously, and gathered himself together to speed away on his bike toward his apartment.

After a while he had to stop, his breath rasping

from the strain of constant pedaling. Dismounting his bike, he sat down on the ground heavily, his body slumping on a curb near the elementary school parking lot. He could hear children playing in the old gymnasium, screams and laughter of tiny voices, and he lay back, propping himself up with his elbows on the freshly cut grass. It felt somehow cool on this hot day.

The sun, its white-hot light heating the blacktop until wavy lines appeared to float just above the road, beat him relentlessly, and his mouth begged for the water bottle that he drained over an hour ago. He closed his eyes and let the sun fall on his upturned face, drying the wetness of his tears.

"Michael?" came a familiar voice, an all too familiar voice. "Michael Prosper?"

He opened his eyes and shielded them from the sun just enough to see the shape of someone standing over him, her auburn hair tied back in a pony tail, her own small hand shading her eyes from the oppressive light.

It was Kalila. Kalila Steren.

"I thought that was you," she said rather plainly. "How long have you lived...I mean...have you been here since..."

"Since high school," he said, his voice a little quivering dog in a corner. "I've been here since then."

She put her hands on her hips, her short sleeve UnderArmor shirt to Michael looking like the color of lime sorbet. A small smile began on her full mouth but then died. He began to move like a man exiting a burning building.

"I...I'll be going," he stammered, his knees popping as he rose to his feet and grasped the handlebars of his rickety bicycle. "I didn't mean.."

"No," she said, a hand resting on his arm. It felt good, like coming home to his mother, like warmth and love and old feelings of magical Friday nights when people used to cheer him on.

An awkwardness fell over the both of them as they strained their eyes in the heat, each of them trying as if to see a younger version of each other that no longer existed, maybe travel back to a day when things were not as complicated, a day before the incident that separated their lives forever.

"Look," she said, her eyes dropping down, her mouth twisting to the side as she did before, that trait not lost with age. "I guess you know he's yours, but I'd really appreciate it if you didn't...you know...get involved. He doesn't know, and I'd like him to think that his dad was the man who died in Afghanistan."

He wanted to say something, but her revelation about the boy, although expected, was still more than he could take in. He stammered for a second, then caught his breath.

"Oh no," he said, almost too abruptly, but trying to be cordial, trying not to re-open the wound. "I don't think he'd...you know...understand. It's ok, really...and I'm sorry about Andrew."

He somehow remembered the name.

"Oh, it's ok," she said, though it wasn't. "It's been

a few years and we've kind of gotten on."

"Yeah. A few years."

Michael could hear the cicadas and the sound of the blood roaring in his ears.

"Well," she said, turning, her eyebrows raised. "I'll get back to work. Those kids won't exercise if I don't make them."

"You teach P.E?" he asked.

"Yeah," she said, a little awkward laugh. "This former cheerleader does what she loves."

He laughed, but he didn't feel the joy of it, simply a gut reaction that boiled out of him as he watched her walk back without another word to the open door of the gym where a little blonde girl in pigtails stood with her hands clasped behind her back. Kalila stooped to pat the little girl on the back and they entered the darkness of the gym just as Michael subconsciously waved at them, his hand flicking back and forth for half a second before returning to his side.

He rode home in silence, the wind somehow unable to dry his eyes.

18: Containment

If mom came home...

Kallie and Danny sat on the couch in his living room, the light from outside very dim through the dark curtains on the windows, superheroes battling super villains for claim of the earth on the flat screen, and Danny knew he was walking down a road that was not in the least bit appropriate.

He could feel Kallie next to him as she scribbled away in a spiral bound notebook, her ragged trigonometry text open, imaginary numbers signified by the letter "i" in front of each of them. He sat very close, his arm around her shoulders, their thighs touching.

She turned to face him, her sweet vanilla perfume surrounding them.

"I think you need to calm down, Danny," she said, her grin sardonic. "If your mom comes home and finds us alone..."

"She won't," he said, scooting away from her a bit and wiping the sweat of his palms on his jeans. "She's got a dentist appointment or something. Are you saying I'm not a gentleman?"

"No," she said, closing the book and placing it on the coffee table in front of her. "It's just...Danny I love you and all...and this past month has been really hard..."

He put his arms around her, and she pressed against him then, her mouth finding his, and they kissed, his hand reaching up to find her shoulder, then the soft skin of her neck beneath her auburn hair, and then he heard a car horn outside and jumped up, nearly falling when the little dog with the cone around its head trotted beside the couch.

"What's wrong?" she asked, a playful smirk on her face.

"Nothing…nothing's wrong," he stammered. "I just thought I heard…"

Going to the window he peered outside to see that his mother had not arrived at home, did not have a load of groceries to carry in, was not there to keep him on the straight and narrow.

It was up to him, and it took everything he had to do it. She had given in to him, but somehow he felt the urge to let things go too far.

Her father was a very large man…and was sheriff.

"Hey, let's go out," he said, his voice still shaking. "What's playing at the Warren?"

She stood, slinking over to him catlike, and both hands grabbed his trembling fingers.

"That accident must have really messed you up," she said, the grin fading away, her eyes narrowing. "Sure. What do you want to do?"

"Like I said. I think I want to see a movie or something, at a theater. Haven't seen one in a while and I'd like to, you know, do that."

"Whatever," she piped, looking around as if she had something more critical to say, but didn't. "Sure. Whatever. Y'think it's ok if I leave my stuff here? Your mom doesn't mind, right?"

He nodded, and she packed things away in her blue and goldenrod backpack. She then went to the bathroom for fifteen minutes or so, but when she appeared, an angel with auburn hair, beaming, they went outside to climb into her electric blue Mustang. They pulled out of the driveway quickly and he found one of the stations on the radio that was not plagued with frequent static and soon they were buzzing down main street toward the outer edges of town.

She pulled into the parking lot of the Super C Grocery, turned to him and planted a kiss on his cheek. He could feel the wetness of her lip gloss there and raised a hand to touch it with the tips of his fingers.

"Where did you want to go again?" she asked. "The movies?"

She pulled out her phone and started scanning web pages. She moved her finger up and down the screen, her eyes rolling up to look at him now and again, her mouth in a twist.

"Man, none of those look any good," she said finally, yet guardedly. "Hollywood has no clue what is good anymore. Just reruns and remakes."

"Let me see…," he laughed, snatching the phone from her hand, and before he could get a good look at what was on her phone she snatched it back with a growl.

"Danny, don't you know it's not polite to do that? Now look. I don't want to go to a movie. I've got cheer practice in the morning and I gotta get up early.

Can't we just go to the Sonic over there and get a shake or something? Save the movie for Saturday?"

She was very evasive, and he just wanted to see a movie…didn't care what. The dark theater, the possibility of…

"What the heck, Kallie?" he said, his voice somehow louder than normal inside the car. "You got no problem sitting at my house and watching a movie but if we want to go out you make all kinds of excuses. What's up with you?"

She smiled the smile of a woman who was about to get her way, knew she would get her way, and then she softened.

"Ok," she said, her eyelids fluttering for a millisecond. "Let's go back to your house after Sonic and watch something on cable or whatever. I'm not really that interested anyway. Doesn't matter about a movie. I don't care. I just wanted to spend some time with you, that's all, and sitting in a dark movie theater doesn't really fit the bill, you know? I mean, you're kind of handsy sometimes, Danny. Don't get me wrong…I just… I just don't feel comfortable."

She put out her small hand and grasped his, but it was innocent, as if taking the hand of a friend, and even though he knew that she still wanted to date him, that they were a matched pair, he wanted more from her. For a moment all he could hear was the sound of the air conditioner vents on the dashboard and the music of some flash-in-the-pan band on the radio turned down to the bottom of the dial.

He let out a breath.

"Yeah," he said. "Let's go to Sonic. I've got a need for a root beer float."

But he didn't want a root beer float. He wanted to go see a movie, and wondered why she was so adamant about not leaving town, why she shot avoiding looks at him with those beautiful eyes of hers, why her mouth pursed whenever he mentioned Moore or Norman. He knew that it was her desire to keep their relationship pure, innocent, and he began to feel guilty for taking them down a different path.

Just a little.

As she signaled and rolled out into traffic toward the Sonic drive-in, its red and yellow sign glowing in the distance, he stared at Kallie, her eyes on the road, and he tried to see her as more than a pretty face, a shapely gorgeous girl, but he couldn't shake what burned within.

19: Corrections

Michael sat slumped in his thrift store recliner, the edges of the arm rest frayed and sprouting the cottony stuffing. He loosely held a battered remote control in his hand, palming it gently, his index finger striking the channel button as he scanned one program after another, each of them from a bygone era, the likes of Andy Griffith, Leave it to Beaver, and a dark grey headed Lucille Ball who, as Michael knew, had fiery red hair. His television did not have cable, and the small flat antenna stuck to the wall with a thumb tack only picked up the digital broadcast stations, all of which seemed to run these types of programs day and night. He had been looking for news, for a sports program, for anything filmed after 1968, but had not had much luck and the strangeness of it had begun to tickle his stomach.

A knock at the door startled him so much he dropped the remote in the floor.

Whoever it was continued to pound until Michael rose slowly to his feet, clomped across the kitchen floor to peer through the peep hole.

It was the sheriff.

With a deep sigh, Michael unlocked the dead bolt, then the brushed steel door knob and creaked open the door to see Norris blocking nearly the entire frame with his thick body. He stood with a forearm against the door frame, his snakeskin boots firmly planted as if cemented to the balcony outside. A toothpick protruded slightly from the corner of his mouth and he had not removed his cowboy hat or mirrored shades so that Michael could see his own reflection clearly like two clones staring back at him.

"Can I help you, sheriff?" Michael managed.

"Oh, no," he grunted and patted his whisky barrel belly. "I suppose I just stopped by because…well there's been a complaint, old fella. It's that Steren widow. She wanted me to have a talk with you about her son and was kinda creeped out that you popped by the school today."

Michael's shoulders slumped and one hand went to rub his forehead and pinch at the bridge of his nose. He didn't remember their conversation that day being threatening at all.

"Now this is just a warning of course. No harm done. She'd just appreciate it if you didn't go near the boy is all. I mean, you don't really have a say in the matter."

Michael tried not to roll his eyes, but did anyway. The sheriff's lips pulled back off of his strangely white teeth, a shark's grin that made Michael wince.

"I ain't seen no reason to talk to you about this, but the widow asked me to. Just passing along the message."

Michael stood in the door as the sheriff turned on his heel and walked away, the dirt on the balcony gritting beneath the iron hard heels of his boots. It seemed like the sheriff might be made from a harder material than flesh, his brown uniform crisp and clinging tight to his brick like features. Michael didn't care. He took in a deep breath and let it out of his nose, feeling the heat of it roll across his upper lip. He tried not to slam the door but he did not succeed, causing the entire wall to shudder and the few pictures hanging on his walls to rattle. He looked through the peep hole to see Norris enter his white truck and drive away as if he had just delivered a pizza or came by to drop off the mail.

Michael grit his teeth together, spun and leaned against the door, tears rolling out of his eyes. What did he ever do to cause that man to hate him so much? He could not remember. He had been told that it was because of a drunk driving accident or something like that, but he thought that an event that traumatic would be stuck in his memory, especially if he hurt someone.

Why couldn't he remember? He wondered if the message was genuine or not, because he didn't remember Kalila being afraid as they discussed Danny. Why would the sheriff say such a thing?

He wiped his eyes with the back of his wrist, grabbed his bike with two fists and after forcefully opening the door he nearly threw the bike out onto the balcony, slamming the door behind him and racing down the steps with it.

He didn't bother to lock his apartment.

He was going for a ride somewhere, anywhere, and he didn't care what happened to him. He didn't care what he did or didn't do or couldn't remember.

The warm wind in his face dried his tears quickly enough.

20: Variable

He turned over again.

The oily, rotten tarp covered his body and his feet stuck out from the bottom like two dirty cue tips. The frayed mattress creaked beneath him and he was glad he had that to use as a bed. It was not far from the way his life was before the red static but it was similar.

Not the same.

The craving had not stopped. The need for the burning down his throat. The need for the numbness that comes afterward. It would be good to have that right now, but he couldn't see well anymore, the blurriness in one eye causing him to display a perpetual wink. He grunted as he turned over again, trying to get some sleep, any sleep.

Not the same.

He tried to talk to the younger about where they were. He looked confused and it was so strange to talk to the younger. Like looking in a grease smeared mirror. The younger did not respond as he had hoped.

Not the same.

He scratched at his beard with one greasy finger, pulled the dirty tarp closer to his face, and tried so hard to cover himself, not let the strangeness of this sun shed its light on him. He thought about how the sky looked all wrong and wondered if what he saw at the edge of the town was some kind of hallucination or dream. No one believed him. No one else understood that it was all…

…not the same.

He sat up, pulled the tarp around him like a shawl, stared at the words on the side of the green dumpster "Noble Pharmacy Use Only" and wondered if the toothache in his mouth was real or an illusion. Grabbing this old mattress, he decided to make his way to the bridge out by the high school, out where the dry creek bed cut a path deep in the red dirt where it didn't run before.

He walked through the back alleys behind the main street storefronts, shuffling down third street past the old middle school, past the rusty old playground, past the low income housing then beyond the high school and over the hill no one seemed to climb. After some time he found the bridge that led to the road that led out of town, or so he thought.

The dried up creek formed a scar in the ground, and the grass near the edge of it had turned a bitter golden brown along with the few trees that rooted themselves there. The leaves had dried up and fallen away, leaving brittle branches which sagged and drooped as if to lament their former green glory.

He dare not go across the creek bed again, not after what happened…what he saw.

He knew why the trees were dying. Dying all over town. Little patches here and there. It was the same reason there were no sounds of cicadas or crickets at night or little sparrows flitting around in branches.

He limped to the edge of the creek and descended to beneath the old bridge that ran across it, and there he found his little table and his discarded pot where he cooked beans when he could get them, and with the sweat dripping from his face he dragged the twin mattress to the shade and lay on it, looking out across the spider web of cracks that covered the bottom of the creek bed. Clumps of long grasses grew along the banks, clumps of purple shafts that looked to him like some kind of bamboo, but he knew that these, too, were not the same.

Yesterday he had reached out to pull at some of the grass and had found it to be quite sharp. It cut him badly, so badly that he had been rummaging behind the pharmacy for something to cleanse his wound. He had found some mercurochrome in the bottom of a little brown bottle, just enough to sting after he had rinsed the cut in a water fountain out behind the high school gym.

He looked at the bandage, holding his hand up between his face and the sun that was not the sun. The heat tried to sweat all the water out of him, wringing him out like a dirty sponge, and he pulled the dirty bandage back to reveal a slash in his palm that did not look as red as it did before.

The purple grasses, each shaft a miniature bamboo but a little sharp on the edges, did not look like anything he had ever seen before.

Not the same.

He covered up his hand with the bandage and

wrapped it around tight, wondering if the purple bamboo carried any poisons or diseases. It happened this morning, so he would wait and see.

The younger had no idea what he was or who he was, and if he knew, if he really knew, would he be able to wrap his mind around it? This was a puzzle that he would have to reason out, to cogitate, to mull over.

How was he going to convince the younger that he was serious about the edge of town and the lawman who wasn't a law man and the other people who walked around this town like the bunch of fakes that they were?

Fakes. All fakes.

Today he had wandered into the pharmacy hoping that he would be helped but they only looked at him with those down your nose looks and those "we know better than you" gazes. This was the only thing that was definitely the same, but even this was tainted with the smell of something that was not like the way it was before.

He sat on the little stool he had stolen from the dumpster behind the school and looked at his bandaged hand and listened for birds that would never call and crickets that would never chirp, and that was when the uncontrolled wetness filled his eyes and he wanted to start over, to go back to where he was young again like the youngest younger and start again, playing football and baseball and going to the dances.

He scooted his stool backward, making little

furrows in the sandy red dirt with the bent rusty legs, and found the shade to be a few degrees cooler than the direct rays of the sun that wasn't the sun.

An engine, revving once somewhere above and then idling, then shutting down, a car door, a slam, and then he heard heavy boots and watched as gravel scattered down the hill toward the dried creek bed, toward the purple grass that hurt so much.

"Hey, there!" came the voice that he knew so well, but hated, just hated. Every muscle tightened when he heard it, and his face became stone.

"Whadda you want?" growled the vagrant, holding his bandaged hand like a wounded ape.

"Just checking in on you, old man," said the sheriff, coming into view just at the edge of the creek bed, his uniform clean and pressed, fitting his thick frame as if it were a second skin. The lawman reached out with one beefy hand and touched the purple grass, pulling back as quickly as he touched it and staring at his fingers through those mirrored shades of his.

"I'm just fine, sheriff," said the vagrant. "No trouble here."

The big man put his hands on his leather gun belt, gripping the front of it with white knuckles.

"I just can't let you sleep under this bridge, now," said the sheriff, his wide grin full of big crooked teeth. "How come you don't stay at the shelter down town?"

"Don't want to. Wanna take care of myself."

The Sheriff moved closer and bent at the waist, as

if trying to see into the dark shadows cast by the bridge. It was like being x-rayed.

"If you don't get down to the shelter tonight then I'm gonna haul your sorry butt to the clink where you'll stay by force. Now what'll it be old man."

"You can't do that! I ain't been drinking or nothin'. Just minding my own business. Maybe you should take note."

The sheriff stepped forward one more step, now standing only a few feet away, within arms reach, trying to be less threatening by folding his hands behind his back, but not succeeding.

"I'm the one who has to make sure the public don't get too tired of seeing your sorry behind shuffling around all dirty and smelly. When was the last time you had a hot shower, ol' fellah? If I were to venture a guess, I would say that it was a few weeks ago."

"Ain't nobody's business about my hygiene. I'm the one who has to live with it, not you."

The sheriff stood tall, his hat seeming to scrape the bottom of the bridge, and with one swift movement reached up and pulled the mirrored shades from a chiseled face to reveal two steely eyes that shone in the twilight.

"It is ever' bit my business, sir," the sheriff said, the voice low and mechanical, the sound of some otherworldly creature, somehow more gravelly than normal. "And I will take you to the station and hose you down if it so pleases me. I am responsible for this town, sir. I will see that it is a safe place to raise our children."

Falling back on his haunches, chuckling to himself at that last statement, the vagrant man put one arm up to shield him from the sheriff's piercing eyes only to feel the steel of handcuffs click around his wrist as he was pressed forcibly upon the sandy ground. In seconds, a thick knee pressed between his shoulder blades, his other arm being twisted around to link it together with the other end of the cuffs. He did his best to struggle, but the arms of the sheriff, iron, as if hydraulic in nature, forced him down so that he could only see the underside of the bridge stretching out over the dried river bed and the strange purple grass with its sharp flattened edges.

"Careful of my hand," he grunted. "I cut it today."

"Yes, I know," said the sheriff, pulling him to his feet and pressing him forward gently, even though the vagrant knew that it was not that gentle, that the sheriff had extraordinary strength. He remembered the last time when he tried to run and how fast the sheriff could move.

Faster than a normal man.

Into the light of the setting sun that was not the sun they moved, back up the sloping creek bank and to the sheriff's waiting truck. He could hear the chatter of the police radio and knew that it was all for show. He resolved that he would not run this time, that he would stay quiet and just go through the motions.

The sheriff opened the door and then helped him inside, and there was that odd smell that was somehow more potent than his own filth, a faint smell that he could not place but caused him to wonder if that was what death smelled like. Yes, it perhaps was what death smelled like.

He sat still, waiting for the sheriff to drive him to the station, ignoring the pain in his wrists and the fact that the wound on his hand did not like being crushed by his back. He grunted, and the sheriff grinned at him as he pulled back out onto the road, headed back toward town.

"We'll get you back to the station and get you all cleaned up," he said, his mirrored shades back on again, reflecting everything around him. "It's my job to make sure you fulfill your purpose here, Mike. If you're off doing your own thing you can't interact. I mean, have you ever thought that if you were to get a job or try to clean yourself up people might not be so scared of you?"

Mike sat in silence, refusing to look at the sheriff, staring out the window at the curbs flying by. No. He didn't want to get a job. He'd been thrown out or fired from every job he had ever held, and then the drinking began, and then the DUI's, and then the long stretch of trips through the revolving door of jail. He took a deep breath, let it out and then he noticed how some of the trees were dying, some of the yards had brown grass, and once in a while he'd see a dead dog lying in a yard or some guy out watering a patch of dirt.

He didn't see one patch of the purple grass, though.

Come Apart

21: Paces

It was the fifth lap he had to run, and Danny's legs felt like rubber.

He passed Coach Wood again who would only look at a clip board and scribble a few notes, and then if he slowed down the whistle would scream across the field.

Danny knew that if he had to run another lap without water he'd probably start cramping, so on his sixth lap he slowed to ask for a drink and Coach's mouth curled a bit as he waved him toward the large orange Gott thermos that sat on an old folding table near a stack of paper cups.

Danny pressed the button and put his face under the ice cold water as it poured across his head and only then did he grab a cup and fill it, feeling the cool liquid wash down his cottony throat immediately cooling his overheating body.

"You need to pay better attention in class and you won't get detention, Danny," growled the Coach, suddenly appearing beside him, dropping the clipboard on the table with a clatter. "If you'da minded your own business the other day you wouldn't have gotten punished. Easy as that."

Danny straightened his back, realizing that his coach was a bit shorter than he was.

"Sorry Coach," Danny said, trying to smooth things over, trying not to think about the weirdness of that day, but it just came out of him. "I don't know. I just saw something really weird, like Mr. DeFord fell over and started convulsing…and…well I'm not sure what happened next."

Coach Wood flashed a wide smile.

"You sure we don't need to send you back to the doc, Danny? Sounds like you're a little punchy."

"No, no," Danny offered. "I guess not. Just… well…forget it."

Danny wanted to forget it, wanted to forget the fact that he somehow had thoughts about things that were just blanks, as if someone had gone into his mind and erased them with white-out but now and again he would run his finger across the paper there and feel faint bumps or impressions that something was missing. He couldn't explain it, and wondered if he should indeed go back to the doctor.

"C'mon," said Coach clapping his big hands together. "Rest of the boys are on their way out from the locker room and we should get on over to the diamond for practice. Get you back up to speed, son! Gotta beat Deer Creek tomorrow!"

Danny noticed his team mates, many of them still fuzzy memories in his mind, faces he couldn't place entirely, a vague blur of a smile or a big win where they were all on the bus at night on the way back from an extra inning long haul. It felt like he was living in a movie, a dream that seemed very real.

They ran to the baseball field, lugging their equipment bags, the team all in t-shirts and long pants, cleats kicking up small bits of grass and dirt from the patchy pasture that separated the track from the diamond. A small kernel of pain began to form at the back of Danny's head and rolled forward to his temples but he ignored it, tried to fight through it, didn't want to let his teammates down.

But it became worse.

Coach didn't let them sit in the bullpen, made them all stand and keep loose, shaking out their arms, doing stretches before everyone started practising their throw on one knee to each other across the diamond. Next everyone ran the bases, practising rounding the bags for a few laps. After a short breather where Thomas and Caleb got lost talking about how Mr. Oliphant wouldn't take late papers, "that old so and so", it was back to fielding the ball, each of them taking their places in the outfield and infield, Coach cracking a few out to them, mostly grounders. Coach handed the bat off to each of them and they took turns fielding grounders to each other, some of them popping them up high left field and center. Of course the two pitchers stood outside the fence throwing into a net. No batting practice for them today. Those guys never did the hard work.

Danny's head felt like it was on fire.

Coach set up the pitching machine and turned it on, all of them wearing helmets, stretching leather gloves over their fingers. Danny's turn came and he stepped to home plate, let one fly by him before getting into his stance, trying to ignore Coach Wood's growl that he didn't try to hit the first playable ball thrown at him. He dug in his back foot, a right handed hitter, waited for the noise of a ball notching into the groove and as it fired toward him he swung deep.

Miss.

"Attaboy, Danny! Show us what you got!" screamed one of the nameless guys on his team. Have to try to remember his —

Zing.

"C'mon Danny! Eye on the ball!"

He set his feet, choked up on the bat this time, squinted at the machine, but the pain in his head felt like someone had the base of his skull in a vice. It made the bile rise up and nearly choke him, but he waited for the tick of the machine, readied his arms, his hips, and swung at the ball.

Ting!

He caught a piece of it, a high pop fly to shortstop, and as he watched the ball descend toward the baseline, the shortstop popping his fist in his glove, Danny bent forward and emptied his stomach contents all over home plate.

As he nearly fainted, falling to his knees, he saw a red mass in the sick on the ground just before falling backward to stare at the blue sky that was somehow not as blue as he remembered it, a faint tinge of purple that didn't quite sit right in his mind, and then faces, several faces crowding around him, eyes wide, mouths open with concern, a sweaty hand on his forehead.

Gritting his teeth, Danny sat up, his teammates helping him by bracing his shoulders, but Coach Wood protested.

"Take him over there, fellas," came the gravelly voice. Danny couldn't see him. "Over there on that patch of grass."

And he was carried, letting his muscles relax as six of the young men held him, and soon he was laid gently on the brown grass, its dry blades scratching at any exposed skin. Soon the Coach was over him, waving his sweaty ball cap in his face. He felt the cool breeze it generated, but didn't quite like the smell of his sweaty old man scalp. His knees hurt him where he fell, and Coach brushed them off with his hands, then he had a little pen light out shining it in his eyes.

"You just look up, Danny," said Coach Wood, and there was another man standing in the distance, just at the corner of Danny's eye, a man who was solid, a block of a man, and he wore a cowboy hat.

"You're gonna be alright, Danny," said the Coach. "It's just the heat is all."

Danny looked again to see if he could make out the man silhouetted in the distance, but he couldn't, only a dark blur at the edge of his vision.

"Look up, Danny," said the Coach. "Nothing to see out there. I need to check out the dilation of your pupils."

He flashed the light again, and Danny cooperated.

"I wanna sit up," he said, and in a couple of seconds some of his teammates were helping him to a sitting position.

He fixed his eyes on the man at the edge of the ball field, and could just make out a face with two mirrored disks for eyes, the rest of his squarish face

128

chiseled from stone and unmovable. One arm was propped against the home plate fence. Behind those shining disks he could sense the man's gaze, feel it penetrate to his bone marrow.

Danny didn't like it.

"Who is that?" asked Danny.

Coach started, stood to his feet helping Danny to his, and looked quickly to the man standing at the edge of the field.

"Oh, that's just Sheriff Norris, Danny. He was driving by when you fell. Just checkin' to see if you needed more care than what we could give ya. You think you need to go the doctor or something? You look kind of pale."

"Oh no," whispered Danny. "I can manage."

But he couldn't.

Danny felt very strange, and when he opened his eyes again he found himself in his own bed, his mother slumped in a chair across from him fast asleep, her head cocked back, her mouth open.

And it was night.

22: Wysiwyg

The sun fell just above the horizon as Michael pumped the pedals of his bike to the rhythm of his own heartbeat. He thought about Norris telling him he couldn't see the boy, couldn't say anything to Kalila, and it twisted in his chest, writhed there like a coiled rattler.

The poison had begun to rise within his mind as he mumbled to himself, his breath wheezing in and out. He thought about Kalila and how she had stared at him, how the boy didn't know who he was, how she told him that he was his father but thought it would be best if they didn't talk about it.

He'd agreed.

But now he was sorry he didn't say anything. He pumped the pedals of the bike, feeling the sweat roll down his back only to be soaked up by his white t-shirt, thinking about how things could have been better, could have been like they were back then when he ran all those touchdowns, made all those base hits, when she held his arm as they entered the prom.

What happened to his life? He'd drank it away, apparently, but that didn't feel right as if he had simply awoken in a place that was foreign, that this was all going to melt away soon and he'd be back in his old baseball jersey, covered in red Oklahoma dirt, sitting at Pizza Hut with the boys talking about how he'd hit yet another home run and the bases were loaded.

A car passed him and turned down a side road, its headlights washing him in a warm glow for a moment. The sun was dipping ever lower as he found the road out of town, and as he passed the green, nondescript sign which read "NOW LEAVING NOBLE" he grinned a bit, but it was a hateful grin, and he looked briefly behind him to squint at the street lights that were winking on.

On he went, pedaling his bike, and as he did he noticed in the fading light that the trees did not look the same out here. They were not filled with the green leaves of late spring but the browns and yellows of late fall. He blinked at this, riding on, but soon he noticed that the grass he passed along the curb near the side of the road was a light yellow mixed with a dead gray as if someone from the electric co-op had gone a little heavy with the poison beneath the power lines.

He had a faint memory of his drunken father screaming about the electric co-op poisoning the trees and bushes beneath the power lines near the side of the road with Round Up, the fears of toxins seeping into the ground water. Michael stopped his bike to look at it because it now looked as if someone had gone way too overboard with it, every bit of vegetation dead and dying around him.

His heart racing, sweat pouring down his face and stinging his eyes, Michael turned to look down the four lane road and wondered where all the cars were. Surely someone was coming home from work or going into Norman about now. The traffic light ahead just over the hill was shining with a deep red hue. He decided to ride toward it.

The hill between his present position and the traffic light was steep, and the air for some reason felt dry and thin, as if he were at a high altitude. He crested the hill and as the gravity on the other side caught him, pulling him down the other side, Michael squeezed the hand brakes, his hands working like mad, his feet working backward as if he could brake a bike like he did as a child.

The traffic lights were buried halfway up in a sand dune and beyond that, stretching out as far as he could see, a desert landscape, wisps of trailing sand blowing like long yellow scarves from the crests of multiple dunes, their crests highlighted by the fading light of the sun. The blacktop four lane road buried itself in the sand just at the traffic light, and just as Michael came to a stop all three of them turned green.

He nearly fell from his bike trying to climb off of it, and he lay it down in the road behind him, discarded. He staggered to the edge where the road disappeared into the sand and squatted there, reaching out and placing one hand on the sand, feeling its strange powdery texture, not gritty at all but like fine flour, and there were strange colors within, iridescent in the fading light, little sparkles of green and purple.

He began to gasp, standing to his feet, rushing to his bike and climbing clumsily onto it to straddle the seat and pedal away, climbing the hill after shifting down into second gear, and when he crested it he saw the lights of Noble shining back at him. He pedaled hard, his legs burning and complaining, his right knee feeling the creeping grind of arthritis, but he did not stop. He zipped through town, weaving around pedestrians and cars, flat-bed trucks and children, until he started again out of town the other direction opposite the grand expanse of desert he had just seen.

He rode on, seeing the trees again change color, the people become less and less visible, until there were not any cars or vehicles or anything to be seen, and when he reached yet another hill, climbing it in second gear again, slowly pedaling, he leaped from his bike, dropping it to the pavement, and with his last ounce of strength walked to the top of the hill, his breath rasping in and out.

He sank to his knees there in the middle of the blacktop, right on the fading and cracked yellow line. Nearly the length of a football field in front of him the blacktop stretched out and then disappeared beneath the sand, and buried just a few feet from the edge was a rather normal looking stoplight, three green lights turning slowly yellow and then red. There was an acrid odor in the air, something metallic that blended with the saltiness of his own sweat.

He stood to his feet, his knees knocking a bit, and he shuffled his feet on the lonesome blacktop, but as he came closer to the sandy desert dunes, the air became thin, sour, as if he were breathing in the fumes from some strange machine. He staggered backward and sat down hard, his hands out behind him to prop him up, but his mouth stayed agape, his tongue dry in the desert air.

He could hear the vagrant man's words in his ears. *You go see for yourself and you'll see the nothing, the nothing that's wrong! Help us both. Go see it.*

The sun dipped just below the horizon now, and he could see again a lumpy landscape of sand, iridescent sand, and as he crawled back up the hill where he could see the town glowing in the distance behind him, he rolled over past the curb and lay down on the dying grass on top of the hill, the moon to him suddenly looking a little too large and a little too blue.

23: Catalyst

He stood at the crest of the hill, the stars now winking to life on a blanket of black. He held some of the strange sand in his hand, a few of the grains sparkling like the stars above him, purple and green. A hot wind blew across his face, dry and absolutely quiet. He wondered why he could not hear anything in front of him as he stared out across the dunes, their crests visible as hazy curves in the strange blue light of the moon.

His mind raced, wondering why the town of Noble, his home town, the town where he grew up, had suddenly been uprooted from Oklahoma and plopped down in the middle of a desert. He wished he could wake up if he was indeed dreaming, like the red static, the oddness of how he found himself in that park, how his life seemed to be not what he wanted, not what he had planned.

The strange odor had not subsided, a smell that made him think about the oil fields where his father had spent a lifetime before dying from…dying from… what was it that had taken him away again?

All the gaps. All the gaps in his memory that seemed to have been ripped out somehow, and the vagrant who had told him about all this. He knew he had to find him and figure out what was going on. Nobody in town seemed to be the slightest bit concerned or interested that they were completely surrounded by a massive desert.

The middle east? The Gobi? Where was he? And how?

White lights washed across the road as an engine could be heard over the faint breeze blowing in from the sand dunes, lights that washed everything in sunny brilliance until turning blue and red, flashing brightly.

Michael slowly turned to see a block of a man step from a white truck, the blue and red colors dancing across the paint and the blacktop, lighting everything up like Christmas, but Michael's stomach rolled over when he saw the mirrored shades and the tall cowboy hat, heard the pointed toe snake skin boots scraping across the pavement.

"Michael," said Norris. "I need you to come back with me right now. Ain't no need for trouble. You just wandered out a little far."

Michael threw out his hands in front of him as if to cast a spell or ward off an attacker.

"Wait right there!" he shouted. "I ain't going nowhere with you. You know what all this is about? Look out there! It's a de—"

"—Yeah, it's a desert, so what," Norris snorted. "Now are you gonna get in the truck or am I gonna have to use my little helper."

In the sheriff's right hand something flashed silver, but Michael couldn't make it out in the strobe of the dash lights. It wasn't a gun. Michael took two steps back and Norris leveled whatever it was at him and gave two flicks of his wrist.

"This thing hurts, Michael," he growled. "I don't

really want to use it on you. Gonna have to make all
this right."

"What do you mean? The whole town has been
relocated to a desert somewhere. Is this some kind of
government thing? What the heck, man!"

Michael saw something green glow on the end of
the silver thing and then he didn't see anything at all,
slumping to the pavement, a bag of sand and rubber.

Sheriff Norris walked calmly over to where
Michael had fallen, his boot heels scraping the
pavement, and knelt down to place two thick fingers
on Michaels carotid. His mouth tightened and he
stuffed the silver thing in his waistband at the small
of his back. Unclipping his radio from his hip he
stood again, clicking the receiver twice.

"Looks like he got brave," said the sheriff. "Want
me to do the usual or throw him in the tank for the
night?"

Something over the speaker whistled and clicked,
something like static but in a mathematical pattern. A
string of numbers.

"Sure thing. You're the boss."

Silhouetted by the flashing blue and red lights,
Sheriff Norris hoisted the sleeping form of Michael
Prosper over his shoulder with ease, lay him carefully
in the bed of his truck, climbed inside the cab,
slammed the door, turned off his lights and calmly
drove back into town.

24: Bug

He sat up and nearly bumped his head on the bunk above him, snagged some of the wisps of hair on top of his head on the springs. Wincing, he reached up to free them but they pulled free on their own. He scratched at his beard. The odor of his own body was no longer the pungently unwashed saltiness to which had become accustomed.

He felt he needed a drink.

Frowning, he blinked his bleary eyes at the bars to his right and the small barred window to his left. His head hurt. He looked down at his hands and at the strange orange jumpsuit, short sleeves, the graying hair on his arms, the fading tattoos. Not under the bridge.

He wondered where all his stuff went.

Tap. Tap. Tap.

"You ready to eat, Mike?" came a voice, a young voice to his right. "High time you did. You've been snoozing pretty good since Sheriff Norris brought you in."

"Ain't hungry," he growled. "And my name's not Mike! It's...It's..."

"Aww, now. That ain't no way to be. Went down to Kendall's and got you a nice plate of chicken fried steak, mashed taters and gravy. I put it in the microwave till you woke. Didn't want it to get cold."

"Ain't. Hungry," said the old man, stroking at his beard. "Now you go on and file some papers or whatever. Leave me be."

The young deputy, his badge a shiny brass as if freshly minted yesterday, shifted from one foot to another and cast his eyes down as if hurt. His smile faded away.

"Well I'll keep it in the microwave in case you change your mind. A body's gotta eat."

The prisoner's hand gesture was not seen by the deputy as the young man turned before it could be seen, and the prisoner raised it higher, using the other hand for emphasis.

The silence in the small cell, thick in the air like oppressive fog, swallowed him whole. He decided he would do just like last time and wait until they tired of trying to convince him of where he was and what his purpose here in this place might be, and then they would decide that he was not worth the trouble, and he would be off again, wandering this town, until he found another bridge to sleep under and await the inevitable.

He was tired of the madness, the uncertain skies and uncertain faces of this place that looked like Noble, that sounded like Noble, but wasn't Noble at all. He wondered if he was missed back wherever he came from that he couldn't quite remember. That was still fuzzy. The whole "before". He tried to remember it but there were gaps in there, and he tapped on his forehead with a newly manicured fingernail.

"I need a drink," he said aloud. "Hey! Could you guys get me some whiskey or something? Heck, some mouth wash will do."

Silence, only the faint hum of the lights above his head.

He lay back on the lower bunk again, crossed his wrinkled hands on his chest, one slippered foot on the floor, and stared at the intricate pattern of interwoven wires and springs above him, the grey and white striped mattress. He lay there for a moment, and then closed his eyes, feeling the coolness of his eyelids, and then he heard a click just down by his feet. It was something he had heard before, an unmistakable click of metal on metal, and he quickly flicked his eyes downward to see a small slot in the brick wall close with another audible click, leaving no trace that it was there, only the painted white cinderblock wall. With a shriek he nearly fell out of the bed, scooting backwards across the floor, his mouth agape, his eyes bulging, his breath wheezing in and out.

"You can't just do that!" he screamed. "You can't just go and stick me with needles!"

He sat in the center of the cell, his arms wrapped firmly around his knees, rocking back and forth, his eyes darting around the walls.

"You ok, Mike?" asked the deputy who was suddenly standing near him just outside the bars.

The old man stood on creaking knees and dusted off his orange jumpsuit.

"That's fine, that's fine," he mumbled. "And my name ain't Mike…at least I don't think so."

"Sure," smiled the deputy. "I suppose you ain't been picked up for vagrancy either. Them was just your secret spy clothes, right? By the way, I tossed them in the dumpster. No use in laundering them. I'll have Marcy pick you something out before you go back to the veteran's home."

The prisoner stood silent, stroking his beard twice, and this time he made sure the deputy saw the hand gesture, but it was sort of slanted to the left. The deputy only raised his eyebrows a bit before taking two steps backward and sitting in a chair next to a small wooden desk. He took a newspaper from the top of the desk, flipped it open, and began to read.

Mike went back to the center of the floor, looking to see if he was exactly equidistant from either wall, and sat down on the cold, grey painted concrete. Before long he heard hard heels echoing on the floor outside, and the deputy did not look up as Sheriff Norris stepped into view, his shades reflecting everything around him, his uniform crisp and tight on his thick body.

Norris slapped the newspaper and it rattled.

"I need you to go check in on subject two," he said, that voice deep as if it came from beneath the floor. "Guy needs to go back home after they're finished with him. Should be fine after that."

"Yessir," said the young man, folding the paper and scurrying away.

Norris watched the deputy leave, a toothpick just in the corner of his mouth, buried way back there by his molars, a sharp, crooked grin.

The door slammed, and the sheriff's large head turned slowly, mechanically, and then he faced his prisoner and took a deep breath.

"You might as well get on up off the floor, Mike," he said, his voice even, a cadence of soft rhythms. "The V.A. is gonna send some boys over here to get you. I'm to make sure you are real comfortable until they get here. Now, Deputy Davis got you some food over at Kendall's and you're gonna eat it if I have to force it down your throat."

As the sheriff uttered the last sentence, the prisoner stood up, balled up his fists, and gritted his teeth.

"My name ain't Mike," he growled. "How many times I gotta tell you. My name ain't Mike!"

The sheriff put up his meaty hands, palms outward, the grin never going away.

"Yeah, yeah. I remember. I'll just stop callin' you that. What would you rather be called again?"

The prisoner opened his mouth to speak, but he couldn't, his lips quivered and he gasped, as if the word was there somewhere but he had somehow forgotten what it was, as if going to the store without a list and forgetting the most important ingredients to a personal recipe.

"That's what I thought," Norris chuckled. "Well, until you figure it out, I'll just be calling you Mike, ok?"

The door down the hall opened again and the deputy came into view beyond the bars with a plate of food and a styrofoam cup and a paper wrapped straw.

"Got your food right here, uh, g-g-g—"

And as the plate flew from his hands, the deputy

fell to the concrete floor with a thud and began to shudder and shake, his arms curling up and his legs writhing around, his mouth foaming and his eyes rolling over white. The prisoner backed up, putting his hands over his ears and muttering gibberish while Norris bent down and pulled the young man over to the center of the floor outside the cell and stood with his hands on his hips watching it happen.

The sheriff let out a long sigh.

The prisoner covered his mouth to stifle a scream as the sheriff bent down to cover the mouth and nose of the seizing deputy with one large hand. He pressed it there, Norris's face becoming stone and his mouth setting into a deep frown. As the young deputy's face turned red, then blue, then ashen white, the prisoner's face became wet with tears, and Mike backed away from the bars to sit on the floor again and hug his knees.

Norris reached behind him and grabbed his radio from his belt just as the deputy quit moving.

"Protocol four-two-three-two," he said as he clicked the receiver. "Please advise."

Static and some high pitched garbled squawks.

A string of numbers.

"Yes," said Norris flatly. "I believe he is not a liability. No one will believe him. I have sent for the relocators. It is only a matter of time. Subject three is incoherent and unresponsive to any compliance. He is having an affect on the others that is worth pursuing. Please advise."

Another string of numbers barely heard through a

volley of feedback and static.

Nodding and then placing the radio back on his belt, the sheriff stood to his full height and wiped his hand on his pant leg.

"It's ok, Mike," he said, his voice calm, deep. "Looks like it was something he ate."

As the sheriff disappeared down the hallway, the door creaking open and then slamming shut, the prisoner watched as the lights outside his cell winked off and a palpable darkness oozed through the bars. Just as he was about to take in a breath to scream, the lights flashed once and when they returned to normal brightness, the body was gone leaving nothing, not a trace, not a drop of saliva. Even the spilled food was gone along with the plate.

Mike stood shakily to his feet, whimpering like a small child.

25: Algorithm

Danny woke just as the sun sent little fingers of light through the blinds covering his bedroom window. He sat up, immediately grabbing the back of his head and wincing. The headache had not subsided very much at all, more of a dull ache that felt like a bruise or a bad sprain, if one could sprain the back of the neck.

He swung around and placed his feet on the floor. He felt an itch on his wrist and when he went to scratch it found a clear plastic bracelet with his name on it and a few numbers separated by dashes. NRH-ER.

His mom appeared at the door, one shoulder leaning against the doorframe.

"You had me worried," she said as she dried her hands with a dish towel. "Could you stop going to the emergency room? I don't think I can handle the medical bills."

"I went to the — you've got to be kidding."

"They wanted to do some CT scans. See if you didn't have a blood clot or something. Turns out you're fine. Couldn't find anything, thank God. You hungry?"

"Yeah," he said. "Sure. I guess. I went to the E. R.?"

She nodded, and there were some tears glistening in her eyes, her face went red and her mouth twisted. He ran to her, taking her in his arms and holding her close as she sobbed deeply into his shoulder. He brushed the back of her head with his hand, her soft hair going through his fingers. She trembled and he held her tighter, then he moved her over to the bed where they sat side by side while she finished crying.

He didn't know what to say, so he sat quietly while she let it all out. As a son whose father had been absent for nearly all of his life he had learned some tricks to navigating his mother's ranging emotions. Some times you just had to let her cry. After a bit, she looked at him, her eyes bleary and blood shot.

"I don't know what's wrong with you, Danny," she managed. "I just want you to be better, that's all. I'll keep you out of school tomorrow. Just promise me you'll not let your grades slip…and no more detention. Good grief, just do what you're supposed to do."

Danny wanted to tell her about Mr. DeFord, but he couldn't remember exactly what he wanted to tell her about the teacher. Something was just at the front of his mind about him but he couldn't get at the memory. It was as if something was extremely important about the teacher, but he couldn't remember what it was. Did he get sick? He just couldn't remember. Something Mr. DeFord did caused him to be sent to detention but he couldn't figure it out. He decided he would try.

"Mr. DeFord," he said, his mouth trying to form some other word, something very important. "Mr. DeFord…he…I don't know…"

"Gave you detention. There. Let me finish your sentence. Why did you get detention from Mr. DeFord? You usually like his class."

"I..." and it hurt to remember, something banged at the back of his skull and he winced with the pain of it. His mother's expression changed, her eyes widening, and she placed a hand on his head just as he jumped up and ran to the bathroom, knelt in the floor in front of the toilet and vomited, the stomach acid burning his throat, his head throbbing with the stress of this involuntary act.

Kalila was soon at the sink beside him, wetting down a washrag with cool water, wringing it out and placing it on the back of his neck, and it felt good, so good and cool. The pain left him for a minute, and she helped him up to sit on the edge of the bathtub. He saw little flashes of red light in his vision, and then she was helping him back to bed. As she tucked him in, just as she had done countless times when he was small, she brushed his hair away from his eyes and placed the cool rag on his forehead, and then she was humming something, something he remembered from long ago but couldn't quite place.

"I hate this," she said, the tears beginning again. "I think I'll have to call the doctor again and set up an appointment. If you don't get better soon, I think I'll have to do that, get a second opinion. Gotta find out what's wrong."

"It's ok, mom," he said, his hand touching her cheek. "I'm sure it's just the stress today, that's all. I just gotta take it easy for a few days. Don't worry."

Danny lay there, his mother sitting over him, the sound of a dog barking somewhere in the distance.

"Where's Bella?" he asked.

"Who?"

"Bella," he said, his face breaking into a disarming grin. "She get the cone off yet? It's about time."

His mother stared at him, her expression blank.

"I...I don't know what you mean."

The doorbell rang and she opened her eyes wide, wiping at her face.

"Wonder who that could be," she said, a sniffle escaping her as she darted out of the room. "I'll see."

Danny remembered the dog. He was able to conjure an image of Bella with the cone that kept her from digging at the wound from the spaying operation. He forgot all about that, however, as Kallie came into his room with a small wrapped package and then set it on the nightstand next to his bed. His mother stood in the doorway behind her and with one soft smile from Kallie his mother raised her eyebrows and then left the room.

Kallie kissed his forehead, then his mouth, then his cheek.

"So glad you're ok," she said, her breath smelling like wintergreen, her auburn hair tied in a long pony tail. "Everybody's pulling for you, Danny. Praying for you."

He smiled, but it was painted on, and he hoped that she didn't notice.

"I think it's probably a good idea that you stay home for a few days. You know. Chill a while. You look so pale."

He pushed backward to prop his head up on the headboard.

"Really?" he said, forcing a smile. "I didn't notice. Is it that bad?"

She rolled her eyes and touched his forehead.

"Heh, yeah. You look like one of those zombies on The Walking Dead."

He lifted his arms, curved his fingers and opened his eyes wide.

"Braaaiiinnns."

They laughed for a bit, and then they sat quietly as his mother turned on a vacuum cleaner somewhere in the house. Danny decided to reach out to Kallie, to try and make sense of the past few days.

"If I told you something that was weird, would you believe me?"

She ran her fingers through his hair and smiled.

"That depends. Does it involve zombies?"

"Heh heh, no. Just… well… something happened to me at school yesterday, or rather something happened to Mr. DeFord."

She stood up, gracefully took two steps and plopped down in the arm chair across from his bed, crossing her legs. Her fingers tapped absent-mindedly on her knee.

"Ok," she said. "If it will make you feel better."

"It's not about making me feel better, Kallie. It's about seeing something I can't figure out, about Grant…somebody…and about Mr. DeFord. I just can't remember what happened."

"Wait right there," she said, her hand flicking out at him as if to wave at a passer by. "Grant who?"

He sat up in bed.

"Yeah, that's it. Grant... Grant Arterberry! I know that's his name. Sat right in there in my living room last week. Got...hurt or something and now nobody knows where he is or even knows that he exists."

Kallie fell back in the chair, pushing herself into the back of it as if to get away from him, her teeth visible through a wincing grimace. It was as if he had found out some terrible secret, one that she had known all along.

"You don't know who he is, do you?" he said. "You've never heard of him, but why do I remember him? Why do I remember Grant Arterberry? The guy was my...my best friend or something....at least I think so. I remember his name and something else about him, about him getting hurt and that's it. Do you know who he is?"

Her eyes began to water.

"Look, sweetie, I just think that maybe your injury might be doing something to your mind," she said. "You're scaring me, Danny. Please..."

She put her hands over her eyes as if to block out the light and he hopped out of the bed, feeling a bit shaken himself, and knelt down beside her, placing his hand on her arm, brushing her hair from her face. She looked at him and he lost himself for a moment in her emerald eyes, their color glossed over by her tears.

He rose to face her, placing his hand on her warm

cheek, then he was kissing her and she was completely falling into him, the both of them falling together in an embrace that was necessary, that gave each of them deep comfort and warmth. But then she resisted, and he pressed forward, and she fought to break free, and he forced himself on her, needed her.

"Danny!"

She wrestled away from him and stood up, sat on the bed briefly, then rose and moved to stand by the door. Danny sat in the chair, sank into it as if it were a bean bag.

"I... I think I'll go for a bit. You can just rest and I'll come by tomorrow."

She turned to go and he reached out his hand toward her.

"Don't..." he managed. "I'm sorry, Kallie. I really am."

Before he could finish his sentence she disappeared down the hallway and it wasn't long before he heard a door slam. In a few moments his mother stood at the door to his room.

"Something you want to talk about?" she asked.

He sat still, staring at the corner of his bed, the sheets rumpled, his pillow on the floor.

"That's a really nice girl, Danny. You should do your darnedest to not screw that up."

"Yeah," he droned. "I guess."

Silence except for clothes tumbling in a dryer, their metal zippers and buttons clicking and banging.

"What was that you were saying to Kallie about some kid you know? What was his name? Garrett?"

He looked at her, his eyes watering, and he let out a long breath, his face suddenly red.

"I don't know, mom. I remember some guy named Grant Arterberry and I can't seem to shake that I know him, but nobody seems to think the guy ever existed. Not to mention I saw something…in school…I think. Mr. DeFord."

He read her face, and what he saw there made him choke down the next few words before he spoke them. He decided to take a different approach.

"I… I think I'll just sleep on it," he managed. "Maybe I'll feel better tomorrow."

"Yeah," she nodded, folding her arms. "I'll just get you something for your headache. Maybe you will feel better after some sleep."

She left him then, and he lay back on his bed and tried not to think about Grant Arterberry or about Mr. DeFord. He grabbed the pillow off of the floor and placed it under his head, trying to relax, listening to the sound of the dryer tumbling clothes somewhere in the house. His mother was shuffling around in another room, and then he heard her talking. He strained his ears through the ringing sound that echoed in his head because of the headache, and faintly he could hear her. He assumed she was talking to the doctor on the phone.

"Yes…yes…not really any change, no. I should give him some of the red ones or the blue ones? Ok. Sounds good. Now you're sure this will work. No. Sure. It shouldn't upset the balance very much. We have to get his baseline back to normal parameters.

It's not really going according to plan. Yes."

The dryer clicked and banged a few times, but after it made a violent noise, he heard his mother say something a little unintelligible, and then a mumbled greeting. There was a long pause, and then she said something quite clear.

"Subject one, protocol three two two."

26: Overload

Beep. Beep. Beep.

A hand sprang out of rumpled sheets to slap at a digital clock with red numbers that read 5:30. The hand silenced the clock, then pulled the sheets down to reveal a balding man, his eyes squinting in the near darkness, his teeth barely visible through pursed lips.

Michael was awake.

"Huhhh. God," he stammered, reaching above him to pull at a chain that switched on a wall lamp. He covered his eyes with his hands, rubbing at them as if to rub them away, and took a long deep breath through his nose.

Was it time for work already?

He sat up in bed, scratching at the back of his head then sliding his palm across the top of his balding head and then down across his face. He propped himself up by placing his hands behind him, and somehow thought about the night before, tried to think about it at least, but drew a blank.

He thought he might have gone drinking again, but was not really sure about it. As his feet fell to the floor he kicked something that rattled, and when he looked down he saw five empty silver cans, all of them bent and crumpled like so many discarded badges of his addiction. He leaned forward, placing his elbows on his knees and his head in his hands, let out a deep sigh and smelled the telltale acridity of alcoholic dragon breath.

No way to live this down.

Something in the back of his mind screamed that all of this was a lie, that he had not drank himself to sleep, that he had not gone back to his old ways. He decided to shake it off, go into the bathroom and shave, get ready for work.

He shuffled into the bathroom, his yellowed t-shirt smelling of sweat, and he found the bottle of shaving cream and a disposable razor. The face staring back at him from the mirror looked like one of those terrorists who have been hiding in a spider hole for a month. Before long he had lathered up his face around his goatee and popped the plastic cover off of the razor when a bright red trickle of blood fell from his left nostril, dribbled down his shirt and splattered in the porcelain sink.

But it didn't stop there.

Soon it was gushing out at a frightening pace, and Michael was scrambling to hold his head back while fumbling for the toilet paper roll, pulling off yards of the stuff before shoving a wad of it to his nose, holding his head back like he'd been told somewhere but somehow feeling sick and dizzy so that he had to stagger over to the edge of the bathtub, find it with his free hand and sit uncomfortably, moaning, a noise that sounded like a small puppy who had been locked in a room for too long.

"Dear God," he said. "What…"

He sat like that for some time, shaving cream dripping down his throat, before he began to cautiously test things out by pulling the tissue away, feeling more warm blood drip down and then holding his head back again. His shirt was becoming a bloody mess, sticking to his skin, and when he dared look down he saw the beige linoleum floor dotted with speckles of crimson.

He thought about cleaning it all up, but his nose continued to drip, drip, drip, and he felt light headed as if he could faint at any moment. Shakily, he rose to his feet and staggered forward, pulling at more toilet paper, pulling a line of it behind him as he exited the bathroom, down the hall and through the kitchen to plop down on his ugly thrift store couch, tilting his head back, until ages seemed to pass before he could pull his hand away from his nose and not see blood. It finally quit.

The clock on the wall said he was late, so he took a quick shower, swearing that he would clean up this mess when he came home, and before long he was zipping along on his bike on his way to Kendall's.

As he pushed his bike in through the service entrance at the back he saw Judith glance up from helping a customer and then back down at her ticket book. Howard appeared at the kitchen door, his apron stained with untold food stuffs, and without a word he strode over to Michael, motioning for the both of them to meet out back.

Both of them stood in the alley behind the restaurant, Howard with his arms folded, and Michael with his hands on his hips, trying to look Howard in the eye but failing miserably.

"Where in God's name have you been?" asked

Howard. "We waited all day for you to show up yesterday, called your place with no response, and you finally stroll in here and expect to still have a job? You realize that Judith really stuck her neck out for you?"

"Yesterday?" Michael asked. "I don't think it was..."

"Yesterday, Michael. You left the job two days ago and we haven't heard hide nor hair from you since then. Wondered if you'd gone off the reservation so to speak, and from the looks of you I'd say you have."

"Look, Howard. I don't know what you think I've been doing, but I'm sure there's a perfectly good explanation for all this."

Howard lowered his gaze, staring at Michael from under thick eyebrows that shaded his eyes.

"Michael. I know what it is to have a problem. I got a drawer full of nine month tokens myself, but you've got to get a hold of this before you end up on the street or worse. I got a whole lot of paying customers in there who want to eat lunch today. You get in there and start making a dent in those dishes. You do good for me today and we'll see what we'll see after work. But I'm done making concessions, you hear?"

Michael could not account for the missing time, but from the evidence in his apartment things seemed bad and probably were worse. He nodded to Howard, touched him on the shoulder, no words able to surface, and Howard managed a wincing smile as Michael moved past him, turning the corner into the kitchen where a pile of food stained dishes awaited him.

Before long, the rhythm of washing, rinsing and drying the plates and glasses allowed Michael to wash away the memories of the past few hours, the eerie voice of Johnny Cash floating out of the speakers in the dining area. It was a song that was not originally his, sung in his deeply sad voice, of icepicks raining on a steel shore. After the lunchtime rush, Michael looked at his pruned fingers and went to the bathroom to wash his hands and apply some lotion that Judith gave to him.

"Gotta let them hands air out," she said with a wink. "Or just use the gloves."

"Gloves get in the way," he replied.

He soon stood in front of the mirror where he ran the small porcelain sink full of cold water after corking the drain with a rubber plug. He dipped his hands into the water and then splashed some of it on his face, feeling it pull all the heat from his skin. He placed his hands on either side of the sink, leaning forward, bowing his head and staring at the surface of the shimmering pool.

He saw a drop of red splash in the center and immediately begin to color it pink. Reaching for the toilet paper again, he pulled a handful from the roll and then pressed it against his nostril, holding his head back, staring at the ceiling.

He saw a small panel snap shut with a metallic click.

It happened so fast that Michael wondered if he

had imagined it, but it caused him to jump and let out a little grunt. Nothing on the ceiling looked like it had a seam of any kind to afford a small sliding door, only a bumpy textured surface covered with dingy white paint and small specks of glitter winking back at him in the faint light of the bathroom. He stood there for quite a while, staring at the ceiling, his hand over his nose, until there came a thump at the door and a clicking jiggle of the locked door handle.

"Just a second," he said, sounding as if he had sinusitis. "I'll be out in a second."

"Michael, we got customers again," came Judith's muffled yet familiar voice, somewhat strained. "You best get out here. Need you to brew some tea."

"Be right out," he said, and when he pulled his hand away the blood had stopped oozing. He wiped his nose again, not seeing much blood there, and flushed the toilet paper quickly, draining the sink, watching as the pink water flushed downward, gurgling on the way out, then rinsed away any bloody residue.

He stumbled out of the bathroom and went to the kitchen to fetch a fist sized bag of tea from a cardboard box, went back to the drink service to set the filter and then back to the kitchen to begin filling a white five gallon bucket full of water in the deep stainless steel sink. He watched as the water swirled in the bucket, and suddenly he felt like he was drowning, looking around him at walls made of glass, and he was somehow in a tank, something down his throat to help him breathe, and someone was

standing outside the glass wearing a white coat, a
metal clipboard in his hand, and before he knew it he
was sitting in the floor of the kitchen, water draining
down a drain in the floor, his clothes soaked,
clutching at his chest as if it were about to explode,
and Judith standing over him, waving her apron as a
makeshift fan.

"Michael!" she shouted. "You alright? You passed
out there for a sec. You want me to call an
ambulance?"

His eyes rolled around, not looking at anything in
particular, and he saw a blurry hand in front of him,
Judith's hand, and he grasped at it, missing it at first,
then she grabbed his fingers, reaching further to
squeeze his palm, and pull him up to his feet, his
knees feeling like they were made of butter.

"No," he slurred, feeling as if he were slowly
falling over the edge of a cliff. "I don't need anything
really. Thanks."

He felt a warm gush on his upper lip, and wiped
his nose with the back of his hand, pulling back a
streak of red blood.

"Just hang on, Mike," she said. "I'll help you."

He supported himself by holding on to the edge of
the metal sink, his hand slipping slightly in his own
blood, his head throbbing, and when he touched his
forehead he felt a large bump that had begun to rise
there. Must have hit it when he blacked out just then,
but he wondered what he had just seen. It felt so real,
as if he had been there before.

Where was that place, the lab coat, the clip board,

and was it a memory or a just a bad dream?

Someone was behind him, and he could feel strong arms wrapping around his chest, looked back and it was Howard, his eyes squinting, his mouth in a grimace.

"It's gonna be ok, Michael," he whispered. "Just relax. I'll hold you up until the ambulance gets here."

"I don't want an ambulance, I said. I'm fine, just...just a little tired is all."

He felt cold terror of going to a hospital for some reason, a reason he couldn't quite put his finger on, but it was definitely fear, just that something in his gut told him to stay away from the hospital, or was it a person who told him this?

He couldn't remember.

God, I want to remember.

His knees became weak beneath him as he fell back into Howard's surprisingly strong grasp. Michael's vision became impaired then, things ten to fifteen feet out becoming out of focus, as if looking through another person's prescription glasses.

And then the red static again, a circular band of it, radiating out from his arms and chest across the metal sink and into the walls. Incandescent lights above sparked and flickered, several people around him moaned as their faces twisted, the static ribbon passing through them and past them.

Judith screamed.

As Michael fell to the floor, his muscles seizing, he saw the crumpled body of Judith lying next to him, her eyes set just too far apart, her nose a crooked version of what it was, her mouth agape.

He felt the world slip away again, and he wished that it was for the final time and that he wouldn't wake from the void that swallowed him, everything fading, fading, fading until silence and darkness collapsed in on his mind, and he slipped away to a place that was cold like the walk-in freezer only a few steps away.

27: Circuit

Kallie parked her Mustang in the driveway beside her father's white truck, pulled the parking brake, and hopped out, her backpack slung over her shoulder by one strap, her red hair in a pony tail that bounced as she walked.

The front door of her home was not locked, and she waved to her father as she strolled across the living room floor toward her room.

"Hey, Dad," she said from her room. "Anything new today?"

"Not really," said Sheriff Norris, his voice a deep monotone. "Just regular business. How is Danny today? That was a nasty spill he took on the baseball field the other day."

She appeared around the corner, strode to an empty recliner beside the couch and fell into it.

"Aww. He's doing ok, I guess. Just a little weird is all."

Sheriff Norris sat on the end farthest away from the girl, his back straight, his hat on a coffee table next to him, a glass of water in his thick hand. His mirrored shades hung in one pocket by an ear piece.

"Weird, huh?" said the sheriff. "I suppose you spoke to him at length about his blackouts."

"Oh yeah. He's been having more of them, and he also says he's seeing some weird things."

"Hmmm...."

There was a pause as she grabbed a remote control

163

from the coffee table to her right and pressed a button, turning on the large flat-screen television that sat in front of them on a small table.

A black and white image flickered to life. A theme song, a monotonous chime of guitar strings, repetitive and yet somehow soothing, overdubbed by the gravelly voice of a man who was narrating. Soon the images of a small suburban neighborhood appeared, and the gravelly voice began to explain about the nice people who lived on Maple Street and that things were about to get very strange for them indeed.

Monsters were set to arrive.

Sheriff Norris took a long slurping drink from his glass of water.

"Did Danny say anything to you about Mr. DeFord?" he asked.

Kallie sat for a moment, staring at the television and the people who were becoming increasingly paranoid of one another, and she nodded her head in disagreement, pursing her lips ever so gently.

"Are you absolutely certain?" he said again, and she felt his breath on her cheek because he was suddenly that close to her, his stubble very visible. Her fingers gripped the brown leather arms of the recliner.

She turned, startled.

"Yeah," she said, her voice shaking. "He didn't say anything about Mr. DeFord. Just about some massive headaches he's having and that he gets nose bleeds. That's all."

He returned to the couch, his heavy body sinking

into the groaning leather, his teeth clinking the glass
as he took another long drink of water, draining it
down until the bottom was very dry. His lips slurped
a bit as he placed the glass carefully on the coffee
table to his left.

The people on the television were becoming
increasingly suspicious of one another as the power
was on in one person's house when it was out in
every other house on the rest of the block. The young
boy who looked like plastic to Kallie told all of the
other people on Maple Street that the aliens look "just
like us."

Kallie's father stood to his feet, collected his hat,
donned his shades and stood just between her and the
large television, his massive frame blotting out most
of the middle of the image, and she began to lean
around him and smile.

"Daddy," she laughed cautiously. "I can't really
see what's going on."

"Can you."

"Really, Daddy. You're freaking me out. What's
got into you?"

As if her last words were some kind of cue, he
reached down, his arms a blur, and grabbed her by
the shoulders, lifting her out of the chair and holding
her in front of him like some type of doll, her legs
dangling below her.

She tried to scream, but his voice, deep and
resonant, cut her off.

"Four-two-six-six-three-two-seven-seven-nine-
four."

Her face, a picture of sheer horror, suddenly went blank, her skin falling limp, her lips drawn down in a dead frown, her eyes two dull marbles.

"What did Danny tell you?" he droned.

"He told me that he saw Mr. DeFord," she mouthed, monotone. "He has no memory of what happened to DeFord one-one. It is clean. He also recalls one Grant Arterberry. He has not forgotten him. He has also shown the pattern of failure in our relationship. The course of events as before seem inevitable."

The people on Maple Street were seeing a faceless man approaching out of the darkness, and he had a hammer attached to his hip that swung back and forth as he walked.

"We need you to let things play out with Danny," said the sheriff, his large head tilting to the side, his dark eyes narrowing. "Let him do what he must do. There is still hope that the project will succeed, but there are many variables."

"Yes," she said, her mouth moving like a ventriloquist doll. "I will obey."

Sheriff Norris then set his daughter down on the floor of their living room where she stood as if she were a planted fence post. He put his arms around her, embraced her lovingly, tenderly, and she yawned, suddenly returning to life.

"Dad?" she asked, blinking her lovely green eyes. "Did I fall asleep? Man am I tired."

"Oh yes, dear," he said. "Nearly fell out of that chair. Good thing I was here to catch you, huh pumpkin'."

"Yeah," she giggled. "I guess. What'd I miss on this show? It looked kind of interesting."

He stood to the side and they both stared at the screen for a moment, watching as the people of Maple Street picked up rocks or sticks or anything else they could use to kill one another. The two of them watched for some time, their faces blank as the suburbanites attacked each other willfully, screaming and shouting in black and white horror.

"I don't know if you missed much, really," he said. "Just some silly show. Why don't you go off to bed. Big day tomorrow. Lots to do."

"Yeah," she said, stretching her arms above her head. "Guess so."

He watched as she went down the hall to her room and then he fit his cowboy hat on his large head, turned on his heel and strode out the door.

The television shut itself off.

28: Cashing

Yes. It was cold here.

Michael's eyes remained closed as he took in a breath, smelling something like the smell of leaves on a summer day, yet the cold was causing him to shake a bit.

The darkness, still palpable and thick even when he opened his eyes, began to fade into a soft light and then a stream of colors, mostly green as a song played somewhere nearby, a song familiar to him from somewhere long ago.

"I'm si-i-i-ngin' in the rain...Just si-i-i-i-ingin' in the rain. What a glo-o-o-o-orious feelin', I'm ha-a-a-a-appy again...."

He felt something wet, a mist that covered his left forearm and that side of his face. It caused him to jump a bit and he reached out in front of him to find a cold bar of something that felt like plastic, and as the light blossomed in front of him, he saw that he was standing in a produce aisle, the soft jets sprinkling the vegetables near him with cool water that permeated the air around him. Before him was a shopping cart containing a clear plastic bag of broccoli, a tub of yogurt and a box of Fiddle-Faddle.

Beside him, a man with kind blue eyes and greying hair on the sides was placing ready-to-eat salads in a bin. He turned, and with a smile nodded approvingly, yet his expression changed to one of concern.

"You ok, bud?" he asked.

"Um…yeah. I guess," Michael replied.

"You gonna buy some veggies or you gonna stand there all day, fella?"

Michael nodded at him, and then he pushed his cart along, at least it felt like his cart. He didn't remember much before waking in this store, but he certainly remembered the store. He used to stock these shelves, the first job he was able to get as a sophomore in high school.

He quit after a year. Can't play baseball and work at a grocery store. At least that was what he thought at the time.

He worried that he was not able to remember things again. Somehow that bothered him, made him want to sit down somewhere, try to think this through. He pushed his cart along, almost as if the cart were pulling him instead. He turned the corner, passed an end cap full of chocolate syrup and toppings for ice cream sundaes, and his cart banged into someone else's.

Kalila Steren's.

"Excuse me," she said without looking at him, and then she looked, and then she looked away.

"Sorry," he said, pulling his cart back a few steps. "I really am…just didn't see you there."

She smiled, not really a smile of warmth but a smile of courtesy. He started to move on, but then turned to her, a sad frown drawing down his mouth.

"So, you come here often?" he asked, sheepishly, pointing a finger at her and halfheartedly chuckling.

She started, as if slapped, but then she pulled her basket back a few paces more and smiled, a line forming between her eyebrows just above the bridge of her nose, a signal that said the laugh was genuine but cautious.

"Is that the best you can do?" she laughed. "I mean, really."

"Apparently," he said, looking at the white tiled floor.

Suddenly he remembered what he did all those years ago in a wave of shaking guilt: the prom, the dancing, the hands groping in the darkness, her protests, and his awful deed.

He had to say something, something worthwhile.

"I'm sorry," he said, his voice low, nearly inaudible. "I'm so sorry, Kalila. I was so wrong, so very wrong. Can you ever forgive me? I understand if you don't want me in you or Danny's life, but please just forgive me. You don't have to, but at least I asked. I'll…I'll leave you two alone, really. Just forgive me."

Her face shifted, the awkward smile washing away to a blank stare, a trembling lip, and eyes that began to water with tears.

"Michael," she said slowly, the words pouring out. "I…I forgave you a long time ago, Michael. We were kids, just stupid kids, and we both were in places we shouldn't have been. There really isn't anyone to blame. I'm just trying to raise Danny with as normal a life as I can give him. If you get in that life, like that could ever work, things might get too complicated. Just…"

She stopped, covered her face with her hands, and rested her elbows on her cart handle. Michael moved to her, placed a cautious hand on her shoulder, pulled back, then placed it again when she didn't pull away.

"I'm not trying to get into your life or Danny's life," he whispered. "I just hope for you to forgive me, and since you say you have, then I think I can live with that. I've made so many mistakes. I don't have a job longer than a couple of months before I go and mess it up. Could be that what happened on that night is still following me even now."

She looked at him, her eyes two pools of green, focusing in on his face. Her hand touched his wrist.

"Stop saying that," she said, her lips trembling. "You had so much to offer, so much you were going to be. Don't cheapen what we had back then by focusing on how it ended. You were a baseball star, a happy kid, a good looking champ, and you had my heart. I know I would have done anything for you. Everyone loved you. Dwell on that, Michael. Don't let what happened ruin your entire life. I've moved on. Why can't you?"

He pulled back from her then, his eyes watering, the tears falling in big drops down his worn face. They both wiped tears away, trying hard to shake off the heavy emotion they were both feeling, trying to focus the conversation back on the trivial, not get too involved.

"Where you living now?" she asked, a cautious laugh emerging. "Not that I am a stalker or anything."

He smiled, a hope of at least staying friendly with the woman who once had his heart in her hands, and most likely still did.

"I live over at those apartments on McGuire," he said. "You know, the ones that are just a few decorations shy of being Buckingham Palace."

Her eyes widened.

"Oh!" she said, her hand going over her mouth. "When I, well, when Danny first came into the world we lived in those apartments. Does it still have that pool in the center that nearly never is clean?"

"Oh yeah. A nice home for the frogs."

"Is the outside still painted in that nice paint chip blue color?"

"Yep. Sure is. A fine example of American craftsmanship."

They laughed together for a moment, exchanging stories about the apartment complex, its owner Mr. Cavenaugh who was rumored to shower only once quarterly to conserve water, and she related a tale about Danny falling out of a tree and cutting his arm when he was seven.

Soon, however, their conversation faded into that lull that long time acquaintances have when they run out of things to talk about that do not touch on the more emotional issues, and that is when they parted ways. Each of them waved to one another one more time, and Michael made sure to get his groceries purchased and loaded onto the basket on the back of his bike before she made it to the front with hers.

She took her time shopping, taking twice as long

as normal, but she couldn't help looking over her shoulder now and again to see if he was still in the store.

29: Repair

Danny looked at his phone again.

No response.

He typed out another hasty text message:

So sry I hrt u. Plz txt back.

He lay the phone on his dresser and sat at the edge of his bed, his hair still wet from the shower, and played with his lip. He could hear his mother in the living room watching television. The volume was nearly negligible, probably so that she could hear what he was saying, listening for her son's words, and he felt like she was spying on him.

That strange thing he thought he heard her say the day before lingered in his mind, something about a code.

The phone vibrated, rattling the few coins that lay beside it, and he picked it up. The message glowed.

Meet @ park. Old place by slide.

One tap on the screen.

K.

Send.

He popped the phone into his pocket, and since he was fully dressed went out his door, down the hall and past his mother. Kalila looked up, her hands pressing into the arms of the chair to get up, and he held one hand out in a forbidding gesture.

She sank back down.

He shot through the door and was on the sidewalk in minutes, nearly jogging, trying to ignore the throbbing pain that had begun to resurface inside his skull. He thought about the last time he saw her, disappearing around the corner as she left his room, the awkwardness of their exchange. He had to make things right. He'd pushed a little hard, treated her as an object and not the person who loved him and supported him.

She was his angel and he had to let her know that.

It wasn't long before he could see the park emerging from behind the rows of houses along fourth street. It was full of old playground equipment that had been discarded from the elementary school when the community put in for a new and improved jungle gym, tree house and spiral slide combination that all of the grade school kids looked forward to chasing each other around. A tall singular metal slide rose from the ground with a curved fiberglass canopy over the top and a long metal ladder, creating a triangle shape. A heavy steel swing set was planted in the lumpy ground, troughs dug out beneath each chain link swing where the neighborhood children's feet scraped and scraped, the seats bowed pieces of chipped rubber. An aluminum geodesic dome, rusting along each bolt, sat behind it all, forgotten and ringed with clumps of dying yellow grass.

He could see her car, the electric blue Mustang. She stood leaning against the driver's side front wheel well, her delicate hands placed on the fender on either side of her, and she was looking his way as he approached. She cautiously moved toward him, her arms folded, and when they came close they paused before an awkward embrace, and then they were standing and facing each other, the only sounds the wind and a red car driving by, a stereo on too loud.

"I'm…I'm really sorry about all this," he said, his voice low, nearly inaudible. "I just got kind of carried away. I've been through a lot and…"

"Stop right there," she interrupted, taking one step back, one index finger raised as if to draw something in the air, her face stern. "I know you've been through a lot, but have you ever stopped to think what your illness has done to me? Who was it that got all your work together from school, defended you to your teammates who dogged you behind your back when you got injured. Look, Danny, I totally get it. You're messed up. You got hit in the head. But can we have things like they used to be? Please?"

He put his hands in his pockets, raised one hand as if to say something to her, then put the hand in his pocket again.

"I know things have been bad, Danny," and she was crying now. "But can we just have one day when we're not recovering from something that you saw that was weird or a day where I don't have to worry that you're going to black out or hallucinate or whatever?"

She began to shake, her shoulders slumping, and it looked to Danny like she might fall over, so he reached for her, took her to him, and she struggled for a second but then gave herself over and they melted together, holding each other while the wind picked up, blowing the heat across them, the sound of the rusty swing set creaking nearby.

After a moment they walked side by side to the swing set, each of them taking a swing, their feet dangling beneath them scraping at the red dirt, swaying gently.

"What do you think is wrong with me?" he asked, squinting at the sun that was dropping lower in the sky, and she laughed. "Besides the fact that I'm an awful boyfriend."

"You aren't Danny," she smiled, her green eyes scanning his face. "You're just kind of weird since the accident and I'm...look, can we talk about something else?"

"Sure. What do you want to talk about."

"Can I just look at you for a bit? No talking? Just... look."

They did, and he took her hand, and she leaned in cautiously for a kiss, permitting him the privilege, and he considered it so.

After a few moments, the sound of creaking chains and yet another car passing by. She took a deep breath and let it out, but it was quivering in her throat.

"What do we do about prom, Danny?" she asked.

"We go, of course. We don't want to disappoint our subjects."

"Whatever," she laughed again. "I already picked out a dress. Dad doesn't want me to go with you. Says... What was it? 'That boy is bad for you, baby. Only wants one thing.'"

"You do a pretty good impression," he said with a chuckle. "And after today you probably have proof that I'm indeed wanting only one thing."

She didn't pull away from him, squeezed his hand tighter.

"I know," she said. "I think you'll be ok. Just take it slow, Danny. I'm not going anywhere."

Words like that were what Danny lived for. They sat in the swings, their fingers entwined, and both of them stared at the dirt beneath their feet, the grass in this playground a dying shade of brownish yellow.

"I just want to ask one more question, if you won't think I'm being weird," he said, not looking at her.

"Ok, Danny, but then we drop it, ok?"

"Sure."

He turned to look at her then, and a hot breeze lifted small wisps of her delicate red hair that waved around in front of her deep green eyes. Her lips parted in a soft smile that told him he could tell her anything and she wouldn't run, wouldn't criticize, but would love him regardless.

"Have you noticed anything weird about our teachers or, like, your dad? My mom has been kinda crazy lately, all up in my business about you and about my friends. She doesn't remember Grant Arterberry but I do. I can see him just as plain as I see you right now. And then yesterday when you left and I was sitting there feeling like a total dork for what I did, she said something from the living room, I think. Something about a string of numbers and a… what was it called?…a protocol."

Her mouth drew down into a frown and her eyes squinted a bit.

"A protocol, huh? Are you sure?"

"Kallie, I'm not lying to you. I don't know what to make of it myself and I got nobody to talk to about it. Please, will you just —"

"My dad's been acting kind of strange," she said.

They paused. His eyes widened.

"Yeah," he said. "He doesn't like you going out with me, that's all."

She touched his shoulder.

"No. Just today I went home and he was there, not patrolling around, just sitting there on the couch drinking a glass of water. I remember getting kind of freaked out by his behavior and then he…"

"Yeah?"

"He…I don't know. He was fine all of a sudden. I don't really remember much about it, but it was really weird."

He reached up and brushed some of the little wisps of hair away from her face.

"Kallie. Looks like more than one of us is having lapses of memory. What the heck is going on?"

Danny squinted as two halogen beams switched on from a small parking lot across the street from the playground, and when his eyes adjusted, he saw a white truck and an open driver's side door. Kallie's dad emerged, his thick frame causing the suspension on the truck to rock as he placed both boots on the pavement, stood and then shut the door with an audible clunk.

They both looked at him, and Kallie immediately began to breathe erratically, standing up and facing him. The sheriff crossed the street, striding toward them as if in a dream.

"Dad, were you spying on us?" she shouted. "Not cool."

He smiled, his crooked teeth a white blaze, his big hands suddenly above his head like she had leveled a rifle at him.

"Oh, no, darlin'," he boomed. "Just popped by to see if you was ok. No biggie. Saw your car parked here and, you know, it's about dinner time. Thought we'd go over to Kendall's."

She let out a sigh.

"No, dad," she said, one hand gripping the chain of the swing, her knuckles white. "I was just talking to Danny is all. I really need to get home and study later and thought I'd just grab a quick bite."

The sheriff put one hand down and waved with the other.

"Hey, Danny boy," he said, his head cocking to one side. "Howz it hangin"?"

"Fine, sir," Danny said, hastily standing, nearly falling back into the swing. "Just fine. You ok?"

The sheriff put both hands on his hips and grinned, but Danny felt uneasy that he could not see the man's eyes through those mirrored shades of his. Sheriff Norris began to stride forward, his heavy steps kicking up small clouds of dust as he walked, and Kallie stood in front of Danny, one hand strangely reaching behind her as if to find him and protect him from something. He placed one hand on her shoulder to reassure her and when he did he noticed that the muscles beneath her shirt felt like a knotted rope.

The sheriff stuck out a hand and Danny instinctively reached past Kallie and took it, feeling a grip of iron, as if he had grabbed a skin covered pipe wrench. The sheriff pumped it twice, and then let go.

"You two look happy," he said. "Probably want to go to the prom or something like that. I suppose that's ok. You planning on taking my daughter to the prom, Danny?"

Kallie and Danny looked at each other awkwardly, her mouth moved to speak, and then she looked at the ground.

"Yes sir," said Danny, trying his best to stick out his chest and raise his chin. "I would like to do that if that's ok with you."

As if in slow motion the sheriff looked at the both of them, their slack faces mirrored in his shades.

"That'll be fine," he said. "I guess we just let these kinds of things play out, huh babe. Part of being a good dad."

Uneasy smiles cracked across Kallie and Danny's faces then, and Danny put out his hand again for the sheriff to shake it, but the big man turned on his heel and thumped back across the playground, across the street to climb into his truck. In moments the engine revved and he backed out of the small parking lot, his tires screeching as he sped away.

As the sound of the engine faded, Kallie turned, grabbed Danny by both hands as she faced him.

"Do you see what I mean?" she said, her nostrils flaring as she swallowed air. "I don't know who he is anymore."

He pulled her to him and they embraced, her head fitting just beneath his chin.

"It's ok," he said. "I don't understand it either, but we've got to figure it out. Whatever is happening it's not just with your dad. It's with a lot of the adults in this town."

They stood silent for a moment, listening to the breeze rustle the long yellowed clumps of grass around the play dome.

"You wanna let me drive us around a bit?" he asked. "Clear our head?"

She pulled away from him, her eyebrows furrowing, a slight grin forming.

"You want to drive my 'stang? Do you even have a license?"

"You bet I do..on both counts," he said. "Why not? I promise not to speed…of course your dad would probably kill me if I did."

They both stared at each other for a moment, trying to find some normalcy in all of it, and then she produced a set of keys.

"Yeah," she said. "Sounds good."

She placed the keys in his hand, tiptoed up to kiss him, and they walked quickly to her car, but both of them thought about the strangeness of the town and no amount of Sonic root beer floats could change that.

30: Partition

Mike's eyes flicked open.

He stared at the springs and zig-zag pattern of metal wiring that held the grey and drab striped mattress in place above him. He stroked his beard and then with both hands rubbed his eyes.

He had moved his bunk to the middle of the cell, leaving little scratch marks in the grey paint of the concrete floor. He was not about to let those weirdoes spy on him or defile him during the night. If he could sleep with one eye open he certainly would.

He crawled out onto the floor and stood up, feeling around on his orange jumpsuit for any sore places or bandages that might be there. He was sure they were going to do something to him or maybe they had already done something to him. He saw a few small things sitting on the little porcelain sink. He approached it cautiously only to find a red and white can of shaving cream, a razor, a pair of metal scissors and a tube shaped electric trimmer.

They expected him to shave.

He went to the mirror and did not like his reflection. To him the man staring back at him was a stranger. He remembered when he was younger, when he played football and baseball, when he was the big man on campus. The man staring back at him looked haggard and windblown, the once glorious mane reduced to a balding pate, his eyes ringed with blood red edges, his beard pepper grey and shaggy like those men on the tube so long ago who had great morals and who had formed a pseudo-cult followed by Walmart shoppers everywhere.

He grabbed the clippers, plugged them into a wall socket, and for a reason that he could not readily find he began to cut away at his beard, huge clumps of it falling into the sink. It was as if someone was shaving a Sasquatch. Before long he had discovered what his face looked like again and he decided he was tired of having long hair, so he cleaned out the clippers and went to work on his head.

He found the scar he had received from a fight he had started after losing his third job to alcoholism and a poor attitude toward his boss. The scar told him that he was real, that he was indeed who he thought he was and not some kind of fake like the people in this town, like that creepy sheriff.

After he had exhausted all use of the clippers he lathered up his face with shaving foam, using the disposable razor to cut away the stubble. He stared headlong into the red rimmed eyes of someone he used to know, someone who had deeper lines in his face than he remembered, and darker features.

He heard a soft noise, like that of an air compressor when it finishes airing up a tire, and he turned to look at the thick darkness beyond the bars of his cell.

Nothing.

His heavy eyebrows furrowing, his mouth forming a frown, he grabbed the scissors and held them with one of the blades jutting out from between two fingers, grabbing tight the other blade, and he grunted toward the bars.

"Whoever you are, I'm not playing games anymore! You come out and face me or do whatever or kill me 'cause I'm done taking it on the chin. You try to mess with me again, you'll get a mouth full of blood."

Silence.

He turned, placed the scissors on the sink, pulled clumps of beard and mane out of it and tossing it in the small metal dust bin in the corner near the stainless steel toilet. He then washed the remainder of it down the sink. He ran warm water over the back of his hand when he suddenly heard a door open somewhere, footfalls, and a squeaking wheel of a cart and rattling metal.

The darkness beyond the bars fled from a bright incandescent light above.

Just into view beyond the bars came a skinny deputy, an albino white headed kid with connect the dot freckles, dressed in the brown and khaki police uniforms of the law of this town, wheeling a long white gurney. He jingled some keys and unlocked the door, sliding it aside.

"What do you think you're doing?" asked Mike, his hand gently twisting the faucet handle shut, moving his scissor wielding hand behind his back.

I can take this dude.

The strange albino deputy let out a sigh, and that was when a second deputy stepped into view, a head taller and about twice as wide as his counterpart.

Mike let out a sigh.

"We don't want no trouble, Mike," said the kid. "We just want you to get on this here gurney and we're gonna take you over to the veterans hospital so's they can get a good look at you."

"I don't know about that," said Mike, his right hand gripping the edge of the sink. "I just don't know."

The other deputy stepped into the room, and if he were an inch taller Mike determined that he would have to stoop to fit through the open cell door. His uniform was stretched across his thick chest and his arms looked like they were about to bust the sleeves of his shirt. The giant only stared at Mike with steely blue eyes that were shaded by the bill of his brown deputy ball cap.

"Don't make this any harder than it is, Mike," said the kid. "My dad used to play ball with you back in the day. Sad to see you in such a sort."

"Your dad didn't do nothing and never met me, and that's the truth, kid. And I ain't gonna do nothing but get myself busted out of here, giant or no giant. And there ain't no veteran's hospital and you know it."

Swiftly and without warning, the brute took all of three steps to stand right beside Mike, his hot breath near the top of Mike's head, and reached out for his arms with vice grip hands. Mike tried to fight, struggled, and appeared to give himself over, voicing a low grunt, and then the big man was groaning, staggering back, one blade of the scissors jammed deep in his abdomen, his big fingers reaching for it, the second blade of the scissors teetering back and forth on its hinge.

Mike jumped back against the wall feeling his face pulse red with rage.

"Leave me alone, now!" he screamed. "I told ya I wasn't going with you fellas and I mean it. Nobody else has to get hurt."

The big man pulled the scissors from his stomach, dropping them so that they clattered on the concrete floor. He seethed, his face twisted in anger, a pale skinned hulk, and he reached for Mike again, and this time the albino deputy produced a small metal device that Mike had seen before which made him suddenly very compliant, putting up his hands.

"I'll use this, Mike," the kid said as he held aloft the little silver disc shaped device in one trembling hand. "You know what it does. Now cease and desist. We don't want to hurt you."

Mike put his hands up, but as soon as he did, he saw the room become wavy as if they were all suddenly underwater, the walls shimmered, and a wave of the red static flowed out of him and slammed into the two deputies. Both of them fell to the floor immediately, the lights above his head sparked, and the bright lights in the hallway outside the cell flickered. Mike squinted his eyes shut because the phenomenon produced a throbbing pain in his head that felt as if a small angry creature was trying to get out, clawing at his skull. He fought through the nausea, reached for the sink to steady himself, and when he could bear to open his eyes in the flickering light he saw the two deputies lying on the floor, their bodies disfigured and burned. Their clothing was singed and melted in places and the sickening sweet odor of burning flesh assaulted his nose.

"Oh..." was all he could manage as he covered his mouth and nose with his hand. He staggered forward, nearly tripping over the grisly remains of the two deputies, wondering when the sheriff would inevitably appear, and made his way to the open door of the cell. Pushing the gurney aside, he shuffled forward, seeing a long hallway beyond an open brushed metal door, spot lights placed at regular intervals on the ceiling leaving large pools of light along the floor.

He followed it out.

Before long he emerged in a darkened room, the only faint light coming from several large cylinders that rose out of the cold shiny floor. The darkness in this room was palpable and he could not see a switch anywhere, but he stumbled around in the darkness, moving toward one of the dimly lit cylinders. He leaned his back against it, feeling the smooth surface somewhat like glass, his hands finding warmth there, wondering where he had ended up, wondering if it would be like before when he discovered the sheriff's dirty little secret.

I can go back to the cell. Maybe they'll stop since two of them were killed. No. They won't stop.

Leaning against the cylinder he felt a vibration, and a sound of something swirling, a sound like bubbles being released beneath a vat of liquid. Out of the corner of his eye he sensed movement and realized that it was coming from behind him, and turning to face the cylinder his eyes opened wide to see the form of a humanoid inside, its legs and arms writhing and squirming, a dark shape suspended in the viscous substance within. He moved closer, dared to inch closer, and saw what looked like a mask covering the face, a mask made from some type of coral or bone. It covered the face completely so that he could not make out their identity.

He tapped on the surface with one knuckle and it made the sound of thumping a fifty gallon drum of water. He took two steps back so as not to disturb it further and fell into someone's arms. He shrieked, spinning around to face a man wearing a white lab coat, knocking the metal clip board out of his hand.

"What are you doing here, Mike?" he asked politely yet without emotion. "You must return to your cell so that we can assure your safety."

Mike shrieked again, shoving the man backward, causing the stranger's legs to splay out in front, his back slamming against the floor. Something was knocked over in the dark, something heavy, something that splashed and hissed, and the man in the lab coat groaned, staggering away in the darkness.

An acrid smell was wafting toward him now, and the floor glistened in the dim light of the tanks. Mike began to move through the room in the opposite direction, feeling his way in the dark, periodically bumping into tall wobbly cylinders with other humanoids in them, some of them small, some of them large, all of them dark forms backlit by unseen lamps.

He had to find his way home, but wondered if that were possible.

31: Purge

Michael was on his bike again, riding home, thinking about the day at work which to him had been a long droning routine. The memory of his meeting with Kalila at the Super C was not going away. He thought about the lovely soft red of her hair, the way she crinkled her nose when she laughed, and it sucked the life out of him. He couldn't wait to get home, to shower, to relax, to grab some dinner. Somehow he felt as if he had been riding this bike his entire life, as if he had simply batted his eyes awake while straddling it, pedaling it down the street toward his apartment. His memories of today were fragmented, a splash of color here, a vaguely muffled sound there.

The sun had fallen completely below the trees and buildings and he felt the heat of the evening air blow past him. His headache was gone at least, the dull throbbing ache that started at the base of his skull and worked its way to his temples. He took a curve just then and stopped for a moment to rest, his heart pounding, and he dismounted the bike by swinging his left leg over to the right side and hitting the hand brake. He flipped out the kickstand with his foot and sat down on the curb to rest.

He didn't see any cars, only the security lights here and there along the street that drowned various houses in eerie blue pools, the darkness around the light thick and inky. He felt unusually tired, and the back of his neck was sore. He sat quietly on the curb, his legs stretched out in front of him, his hands in the dead grass behind him, and that was when he noticed the leaves.

His hands touched something crisp and when he grabbed at them they crumpled in his hands, brown dead things that had the consistancy of parchment. Even though it was supposed to be spring time, the trees visible at the edges of the security lights looked as if their leaves were nearly gone. Small piles of them lay in the yard nearby, but he couldn't remember them turning brown just this morning. Many of them were green on his way to work, some brown patches here and there in the grass, in various yards, mostly because of the heat he imagined.

He stood to his feet and looked at the grass, saw that it was a pale shade of yellow, the color of harvested straw. In some places, seen in the dim light of the bluish overhead lamps, large brown patches of dark brown dirt could be spotted here and there across the lawn in front of him.

Michael straddled his bike again, and hearing a hissing sound he spun his head, startled by the noise, and a manhole in the middle of the intersection began to produce a strange white steam or smoke. He could hear the sound of grunting and coughing, and the heavy iron plate jumped once and then slid aside, and a figure in white burst forth from the hole in the pavement, falling to one side and rolling over onto its back, the torso lying on the blacktop, the legs just below the knees dangling down into the void.

Climbing off of his bike, Michael looked to the left and then the right before creeping over to the person who struggled to right himself, rocking back and forth as if to work up the momentum to rise, arms akimbo and flailing about erratically.

Michael let out a small whimper when a face, disfigured by some type of chemical, turned to look toward him, the hair on one side burned completely away, the eye socket empty and bleeding, the skin burned and blackened.

"Zero-two-three-six-five-nine-two," slurred the man in a very monotone voice, a voice that gurgled and spat blood. Again, he whined: "Zero-two-three-six-five-nine-two," and then collapsed, a sound of air escaping his lungs, a cough of fluid sputtering out of his misshapen mouth.

"Are you ok?" Michael managed before squatting beside the man to touch his arm, only to pull back his hand from a burning sensation in his finger tips. Something had been thrown on this man like acid or some other noxious chemical. Michael stood, wiping his fingers on his pants leg, looking around, backing up, his head shaking back and forth.

"No way am I gonna deal with this right now," he said, his voice cracking. "No way."

He climbed on his bike, and without pulling up the kick stand pedaled away, looking back behind him, his eyes round as golf balls, his mouth an open frown. He could hear the voice of the sheriff in his ears, asking questions like before, asking about where he had been, and had he been drinking.

194

The man in the street groaned, crawling across the pavement with one arm propelling him, his dead legs dragging behind him, spewing out the strange string of numbers that was an utter mystery to Michael, and Michael pedaled hard, his face feeling the hot evening wind blasting into his eyes, the tears running back across his temples. He was trying to put as much distance between himself and the man as possible, hoping that what he saw was just a dream or a product of his fatigue.

He heard a scream far behind him, and he turned to look again, but before he could turn back around he hit a pothole and went over the handlebars of his bike, crumpling to the pavement like a helpless doll as if made from jointed rods and dirty rags. His felt a sharp pain in his wrist, and he had scraped the side of his arm trying to shield his face from hitting the ground. He rolled over on his back and felt something pop near his waist, a muscle or a joint suddenly out of alignment. He wondered if he could get up, worried that a car would come by and run him over in the dark.

He lay still for a moment before the moaning started, and he realized that he was not far from the intersection where the man had crawled from the manhole.

He could still hear him, muffled in the distance, the scraping of a belt buckle on the pavement, the soft grunting when he pulled himself along, and he was getting closer, inching closer in the dark. Between the intersection and where he now lay was a pool of light from a nearby security lamp, and just at the edge of it he saw a white sleeved arm reach out, grasp at the ground, pull forward, exposing the injured man's mangled face in the dim blue light.

"Zero-two-three-six-five-nine-two," the injured man stammered, dragging his burned body forward, his battered head lolling from one side to the other as he crawled.

Michael rolled over on his stomach, trying to push himself to his feet, but something in his right knee didn't work properly and he stumbled. He looked around for his bike but did not see it in the fading twilight. He gasped, finally making an effort to stand that caused him to wrench his knee and nearly fall before someone caught him, pulling him close. He wore an orange jumpsuit and in the darkness Michael thought he might be looking in a mirror, but he was somehow older, more grizzled, as if life had driven him down a long road, dug a deep grave, and then buried him in it.

"This way," he said, his breath heavy, a faint wheeze escaping. "We gotta get outta here, you and me. All of us. Gotta find a way out."

Michael followed, helped along by this stranger who didn't feel so strange.

32: Malware

Danny opened his eyes slowly, the light causing vague shapes to become solid. Lying on the floor of his bedroom was a small white plastic cone and he struggled to remember what it was for. Somehow he felt a little sad.

He lay in bed, but he had been awakened by the fire alarm in the hallway, its incessant beeping a shrill warning of impending danger from possible fire.

He started, his feet thumping to the floor, and he stumbled out into the hallway with one leg in his jeans, his red t-shirt in his right hand wadded up into a sloppy ball, and he saw a thin haze of gray smoke moving along the ceiling, carrying with it an odor of melting plastic. His mother appeared at the end of the hall, a metal spatula in hand.

Her eyes were not right.

"Hey, pal," she said, one corner of her mouth trying to manage a smile, the other side somehow afflicted with something like Bell's Palsy. "I am making breakfast. Come on in the kitchen."

As Danny rounded the corner, the alarm still beeping, he saw that she had several pans out on the stove, and each one contained a bubbling, melting plastic container, a small portion of the fumes wafting up and into the ventilation hood which was going full blast.

She walked to the stove, bent over the smoke and breathed in, coughing, spraying a fine mist of blood that sizzled and popped. She turned to face him, blood trickling down her ruined mouth.

"I hope you like pancakes," she said, her voice a slow drone. "I've been up since five making them."

He quickly stretched his shirt over his head and pulled it down to his waist, fitting his arms through and then darting to the stove to turn off all of the burners, the plastic bubbling and searing. He reached for his mother who put up her hands and tried to smile, but it appeared as a twisted grin that resembled the melting containers in the skillets and pots. Danny's breathing became audible.

"I'm a little disappointed, Danny," she mumbled, sitting down at the table. "I hoped to make you a fine breakfast. I just, I just don't know what's wrong. Something is wrong. Two-six-four-two-two."

The table, littered with nearly every condiment jar imaginable, many of them open, tipped over, spilling on the yellow flower patterned table cloth. Danny began to tear up and look forlornly at his mother who was now playing with a fork, using it to tear a jagged hole in her yellow dress, goring her leg.

Danny grabbed her arm, but when he did, she kicked away from the table, fell to the floor and began to seize, her arms and legs flopping erratically like a fish that had been dropped on a dry riverbank. Her eyes, two white bloodshot orbs, twitching and rolling.

"Mom!" he screamed, reaching for her. "Mom… oh my God Mom!"

Thump. Thump. Crash!

Danny's head spun as if on a swivel to see the front door to their house bang open and the thick form of the sheriff bounding through, his hands out in a defensive posture, his mirrored shades beneath the brim of his big cowboy hat reflecting the room. He stopped just on the other side of the table, took off his shades, put his large hands on his hips and sucked a bit of air through his teeth.

"Looks like we got a problem here," he said matter-of-factly. "A crying shame."

With tears flooding his eyes, Danny looked at the sheriff, his hands shaking before balling up into tight fists.

"What the heck, man," he stammered.

"This is a real shame," he replied coldly as Kalila slowly stopped seizing and lay perfectly still, a gasp escaping her blood stained lips. "When did you notice something was wrong?"

Danny started and then squatted to the floor, reaching out to take his mother's limp hand. He felt for a pulse, couldn't feel one, felt her neck, started to shake, and then the sheriff was squatting on the other side of her, looking directly at him.

"Need to take care of this, Danny," he said, the white of one eye a solid shade of blood red. "Gotta do my job, what I was made to do."

The sheriff stood, quickly grabbed Kalila's ankles and began to drag her toward the shattered door, kicking the table over with one swift motion. Danny reacted, grabbing at the thick wrists of the law officer, but found them to be like steel rods, the skin covering them feeling like thick rubber.

"I know you don't understand, Danny, but things will be fine, soon. Have to make sure things run properly."

"Let her go, you freak!" Danny screamed.

He spun to pick up an iron skillet from the stove, whirled back around and swung it at the sheriff's large head, only to be blocked by the big man's arm, the plastic flying across the room. Unfazed, the sheriff continued to drag Kalila across the rose colored ceramic tile, a small trail of blood leaking out of her mouth. Danny grabbed his mother's arms and with tears flooding out, his mouth forming a tight grimace, he pulled, but was only helping the sheriff carry her toward the door.

"It is not really necessary to help me, Danny," said the sheriff calmly. "I really do have this in hand."

"Daddy, what are you doing?" came the voice of Kallie who stood in the door, her backpack dropping to the ground, her eyes wide.

As the sheriff turned to see his daughter in the doorway, Danny made his move. He charged the sheriff, and with all of his strength punched the thick man in the ribs, his other fist swinging around for a haymaker. The sheriff took it, and it seemed to Danny that he had just struck the side of a metal barn. There was a thump each time, but it made little difference, and the sheriff did not resist, simply dragging Danny's mother further toward the doorway. Danny scrambled toward him again, grabbing the sheriff's gun from its holster, falling back against the wall. He leveled the Glock at the sheriff and pulled the trigger.

Click.

He pulled again

Click. Click. Click.

"You need to calm down, Danny," said Norris. "This will all be over soon. We mean you no harm."

The sheriff pulled Kalila up from the floor and

slung her over his shoulder like a sack of chicken feed, her mouth lolling open, her eyes closed. Turning toward his daughter, the sheriff narrowed his eyes.

"Two-seven-three-two-four-six," he said, and as Kallie froze, her eyes going glassy, he stalked past her and out to his truck, threw Kalila's limp body in the bed, climbed in, slammed the door, and drove away tires screeching.

Danny sat sobbing, his shoulders slumped against the wall, scooting toward it to try to stand but not able to, the madness of the last few minutes driving him to hysterics. He wiped his eye with his wrist, still holding the useless pistol. His knuckles hurt, his eyes hurt, and he wiped his nose with his other hand only to see a crimson sheen on his index finger.

He stayed like that for some time, the hot wind from outside blowing down the foyer hallway toward the kitchen, Kallie standing stiff with hands at her sides, and then she flicked her eyelids, took a deep breath, and ran to him, sitting on the hardwood floor of the hallway.

"What's wrong, Danny?" she said, her eyes watering with worry. "Oh my God, Danny."

"Your dad," he said, his voice cracking. "Your dad took my mom."

33: Save

At first Michael thought he was staring at a steam covered mirror, the condensation from the hot water of a shower obscuring the image, but then his eyes cleared and he saw a bald man, his beard shaven away, his eyes somehow familiar, and then the memory clicked.

"You," he whispered. "What the…You are that guy on the street…"

"Mike, I guess. You can call me Mike," said the old man, his breath rancid and sour. "Glad to see you are awake and ok."

They had made it on foot to Michael's apartment, and now the vagrant was pacing the floor. Mike went to the window of Michael's bedroom and peered through the blinds at the ground below.

"Wonder if he knows we're together like this," said the vagrant, rubbing the back of his bald head. "No telling. Gonna mess things up for sure. Sun's coming up. Gotta make our move."

Michael sat on his bed, looking around the floor at the discarded beer cans, knowing deep within that he had not placed them there. He thought about the disfigured man in the lab coat shambling toward him, the strange mumbling that came from Mike as they shuffled to his apartment, and he wondered what Mike knew that he didn't.

"I gotta come clean, bro," said Mike, his face a strange mix of emotions. "I gotta tell you the truth about everything. What I saw."

"Look, man. I don't know anything about all this. Sure, things are weird, and I can't explain what happened last night, but…"

"But nothing!" Mike exclaimed. "There's a lot going on here that you just don't get, but when you see it, you'll get it."

Mike paced back and forth, and Michael suddenly realized that he may have a madman in his apartment with him, and that caused his stomach to flip over once. The guy was stomping around, criss-crossing his bedroom floor, his fingers twitching uncontrollably from fists to open hands.

"Ok, bro," said Michael, trying not to let his voice waver. "I understand you are pretty upset about something, but I'm sure we can work out whatever it is."

"No. You don't get it. Did try to leave town? Notice anything strange?"

Michael sat on the bed and scooted toward the headboard a bit.

"Not really," said Michael. "I haven't really been outside of town in a while, not that I can remember. What do you mean?"

"It's a desert, man. A desert as far as you can see. They tried to wipe it from me, but they failed. Something about my brain being too old or something…or the alcohol abuse…, something about…I don't know…widgets and whatnot."

Mike stormed out of the bedroom, disappearing down the hallway. Michael heard a gravelly clearing of a throat and then saw the old man's bald head pop around the corner.

"You coming?" he growled. "Got something to show you."

Michael's feet hit the floor and he reluctantly followed Mike into the kitchen where Mike began to rifle through the junk cabinet, pulling out a ball cap, a small picture frame, and something silver, the locket, the silver locket.

"'Member this hat?" he said, shaking it in the air like a talisman. "'Member how you used to play baseball? 'Member how you used to hit home run after home run, then you messed up with the girl and everything went to pot?"

"I…I used to play a little baseball in high school, yeah, but what's that got to do with anything?"

"How 'bout this boy?" Mike said, holding up a picture of a small child sitting on a tricycle. "What do you know about him?"

Michael took the picture from the old man, held it in his hands carefully, and handed it back.

"That's me when I was little," Michael said. "Don't really know what this trip down memory lane is about."

The old guy sighed, cleared his throat again, and handed the locket to Michael.

"Open it."

"What for?"

"Open it."

Michael used his thumbnail to open the small disc shaped locket. Inside he found the picture again, that picture of Kalila when she was young, her hair in a pony tail, her blue and goldenrod cheerleading uniform now faded with time.

"Yeah," he said. "So we're drudging up the past here and you want me to think about the bad stuff I've done, right? Well, I don't want to revisit the past, old man. I don't want to talk about it, and I don't really care."

"That's the problem. You don't care. They *make* you not care. They put you in one of them vats down under the ground and make you not care so's they can gather their information. There's an invasion coming, bro and you better get it together. You and me are the guinea pigs in this little experiment of theirs and we'd better start fighting if we plan to save everyone. They have big plans, man, I know it."

Michael actually laughed a bit, but after seeing the old guy's face twist and his eyes open wider, he stifled it.

"What do you mean about vats?"

"I seen it," said Mike. "I seen the vats down under the ground. They was going to put me into one until they figured out that whatever they do to us, to our memories, don't really work on me. I always get away, 'cause they don't see me as a threat, but they probably will now. Something is breaking down, the system, just don't know what yet. They got Kalila and the girl, brought us here for some reason. Can't explain it. I figure two's better than one. See, we're connected, you and I. So is the boy, but can't explain it, put it into words. God, it's so weird seeing you both, seeing us both. I guess it's —"

There was a thump at the door and both of them stared at each other.

"You get it," said Mike. "I'll hide. Just don't let them in. If it's the sheriff we'd better get ready to run."

Michael didn't like Sheriff Norris that much either, but didn't see him as a threat, only a bully. The thump came again at the door, but this time it was much more faint. He looked through the peep hole and didn't see anyone, unlocked the door and opened it, and Kalila Steren fell through onto the threshold, her blood stained mouth gasping, her left eye full of blood.

Michael pulled her into the apartment as Mike dashed to shut the door and twist the dead bolt. Her head was lolling around, her mouth agape, her eyes wide, breathing erratic. She managed to get to her feet as Michael helped her to the couch.

"Michael," she whispered, her voice shaky. "The sheriff. He's after me. I...I blacked out this morning when I went to make breakfast for Danny. Woke up in the back of his truck. The sheriff somehow slumped over and hit a tree...luckily he wasn't going that fast, but I fell out on the ground. Walked here, but..."

"Kalila," Michael said, holding her hand, brushing her red hair from her green eyes. "I'm here. Just calm down. It's ok."

"No it's not!" she stammered, her lip quivering. "He's on his way here. Could see him behind me. All the people in the town...on the street...wouldn't talk to me…like I didn't exist….What is going on?"

And she closed her eyes, one bloody tear rolling down her temple.

"Kalila!" Michael screamed. "Kalila!"

Mike put a finger to her throat, paused, nodded his head.

"She'll be ok," he said. "But we gotta go. That guy will be here soon. Seen it before. He kind of cleans up."

There was a faint sound of a voice, somewhere far away, and Mike went to the window over the sink to look out.

"It's him," Mike said, his mouth agape.

Michael ran to the window and looked down at the parking lot.. Limping across it was Sheriff Norris, stopping once to look up toward the window right at them, and then he proceeded to move forward mechanically, his booted foot scraping the pavement.

"Be up there in just a second, Mrs. Steren!" he shouted, his booming voice echoing against the walls. "Nothing to worry about. Just have to get you to a hospital."

"We gotta get out of here!" Mike said, and Michael did not hesitate. They scrambled to grab Kalila just as the door began to rattle with the heavy knock of the sheriff's iron fist.

The door rattled again, pounding and shaking, and a huge fist crashed through the metal near the doorknob, the edges of the hole blossoming outward in jagged lines. The hand slowly pulled back through the hole and then the hard face of Sheriff Norris looked through, the white of one eye covered in blood, dripping down his chiseled face. The hand reached through to undo the deadbolt and the lock on the knob, and he strode inside, one heavy boot bumping on the floor, one foot scraping, the boards beneath creaking with his weight.

He limped through the apartment, his head turning, his arms swinging, his tall cowboy hat perched on his large head. He checked every room, searching in the bathroom where a blood speckled sink and fogged mirror greeted him, until he reached the bedroom where the hot wind from an open window caused the hastily raised and damaged blinds to bang in a steady rhythm.

He let out a sigh, cracked his knuckles, and limped down the hall and out the broken front door.

34: Rogue

Danny, after wresting the keys from Kallie, jumped into her Mustang against her protests, but she managed to climb into the passenger seat as he nearly peeled the rubber off of her tires backing out of the driveway.

"What is up with your dad?"

"I… I don't know what you mean? What happened?"

He stared at her, his face made of steel, eyes shifting between her and the road.

"Your dad is…like…I don't know…some kind of freaky monster is what."

Tears began to roll down her face again.

"My dad is the law in this town, Danny. He'd never hurt anyone at all."

"I don't know how to break this to you, Kallie, but after my mom had a total meltdown this morning your dad came busting through the door and then carried her outside claiming that he was trying to fix something…I don't know what that means, but all I know is that I gotta find her. Kallie, she looked dead."

He tried not to cry again and shifted down as they

rounded a curve, his watery eyes scanning the driveways and side streets.

"Ok, Danny," she said, her hand gripping the arm rest. "I can understand that you are upset, but I didn't see any of that and I was right there."

"Yeah," he chuckled maliciously. "You didn't see anything 'cause he put you under some kind of spell or something. What was with those numbers he said to you? Two-three-seven-two —"

"Stop!" she screamed, grabbing his arm. "Don't say that."

"Why?"

"Just don't. Just don't say those mmmm… I don't feel so good. Oh Danny, I'm gonna be sick! Pull over…"

And she held her hand over her mouth just as he slammed on the brakes. She popped the door open and almost didn't make it past the curb, vomiting on the dead yellow grass.

"You ok, Kallie?"

She didn't answer.

"Kallie?"

She wiped her mouth, but when she turned to face Danny there was a faint crimson dot just beneath her left nostril.

Her cheek twitched.

"Something is wrong, Danny. I think I should go home. Take me home."

"Just get back in the car, Kallie. Get back in the car."

Silently she complied, an index finger dabbing at her nose and coming back with a spot of blood. She shut the door and they continued on, but all Danny could think about was his mother. He had to find his mother.

A few blocks down and they saw a white truck on the side of the road, angled off to the left, its front end crumpled by a sturdy tree that was losing all of its leaves.

"My dad's truck!" screamed Kallie. "Stop! Stop! Stop!"

Danny slammed on the brakes again and she barreled out of the car, running toward the damaged pickup truck, steam rising from underneath the crumpled hood. Danny rolled forward, coasting along until he could roll down a window and watch as Kallie looked all around the truck.

"Where is he?" she said, her arms folding across her chest as if she were cold in this unbearable heat.

And it was hotter, somehow it seemed like the heat of summer had descended on the town, but all the vegetation everywhere was preparing for winter, dead leaves blowing in the hot wind.

"Get back in the car," Danny said. "Let's see if we can find them."

He knew he had to have her with him, had to convince her about her father. She was not safe with that monster.

She walked around the car and when she came close to the passenger side door, Danny caught a glimpse of something to his left, and suddenly a huge fist was reaching through the open window and grabbing him by the shirt.

"Gotta clean all this up, Danny," said the sheriff, his left eye oozing blood from under his mirrored shades. "Don't mean you any harm at all."

"What did you do with my mom, you dip!"

"She is not factored into the equation at the moment. She will be returned to you. Don't worry yourself."

Danny screamed. Kallie, not noticing her father until now, pulled open the passenger door and then slammed a palm down on the roof.

"What are you doing!?" she shouted.

"Nothing to see here, dear. Two-four-seven-three-"

"Kallie hold your ears and get in!" screamed Danny.

She did as she was told, and the sheriff pulled on Danny's shirt until it tore and Danny shifted the car into first and popped the clutch just as Kallie climbed in, her door barely closing in time. The tires screeched and a piece of Danny's shirt went with the sheriff as they rocketed away, the force of acceleration slamming Kallie back into her seat.

"What was he trying to do?" she shrieked. "Danny why was he trying to pull you out of the car?"

"I told you, Kallie," he said, his voice shaking as he continued to shift gears and screech around corners. "Your dad is a freak."

It didn't stop her tears, and she sobbed as they sped toward the center of town and main street. Danny was still looking, desperately scanning the streets for his mother, his neck throbbing where his shirt nearly choked him before it tore.

"Where is she?" he exclaimed.

"I don't know, Danny," she groaned. "Just take me home."

He looked at her again, his face a grimace.

"Are you serious right now? Did you not see what your dad just did? The guy is a total tool!"

She folded her arms and looked out the window, and just as she did, something slammed into them from behind.

Danny looked in his rear view mirror to see the wide face of the sheriff behind the wheel of a commandeered car, and he was gaining.

"Hold on," Danny said.

He shifted down, gained speed, and rocketed through town, the engine of the Mustang roaring as he weaved his way through cars, taking out the bumper of a small compact, yet the driver did not seem to care, the people on the sidewalks continuing on their way as if a reckless teen was not careening down main street with a mad policeman on his tail.

They were jarred again as the car was bumped from behind, the Ford Taurus station wagon the sheriff drove a remarkable match for the speed of the Mustang.

"Where are you going?" asked Kallie, gripping the seat and the arm rest, her arm muscles taut, her eyes wide.

"Out of this stinking town," he growled. "I'll get somewhere I can hide and then come back for my mom."

They were moving faster now, rolling over the top of a hill that overshadowed the town, and now the road was vacant, a full four lanes without a car in sight, so he plowed on, pressing down on the accelerator until the tachometer revved high and the engine screamed.

"Slow down, Danny!" screamed Kallie, and then he did, but not because she told him to. The brakes tried hard not to lock up as he pulled the emergency handle and they skidded to the edge of the road where a vast sea of sand dunes lay before them, the stop light buried half way in the sand just beyond where the road ended.

"Danny, I don't feel so g-g-g-g-."

And she began to convulse, her eyelids fluttering over the whites, her mouth opening and closing, her arms and legs jerking in spasms.

"T-t-take me h-h-ho-o-o-…"

He didn't need to hear any more. Danny slammed the emergency brake lever into the console, shifted into first, and peeled a strip of rubber as he turned the car around in a loop, fish tailing back toward town, trying desperately to keep the car on the road. However, just as he topped the hill, he saw the sheriff barreling toward him, and when Danny tried to swerve around him, the car lost control, and he was soon in the air, spinning and rolling, Kallie falling over into his lap where he held her close to him as the world spun round and round.

He murmured out a prayer as the car hit the

ground, twisting and rolling until it lay on its roof, the tires still spinning.

35: Cut & Paste

Mike moved ahead of Michael as he helped Kalila along, the both of them limping after Michael had landed awkwardly from their second story window jump onto the roof of a delivery truck parked behind his apartment.

"We gotta find something to drive," Mike said. "Gotta get out of here, find our way home."

"Wait," whispered Kalila, then louder. "Wait. We need to find Danny. I was…was…"

"Just lean on me, Kalila," said Michael, holding her around the waist for support. She could barely stand. "We'll find Danny."

"That's all part of it, Michael," said Mike. "We'll need the boy. It's gotta work out that way."

"What do you mean?" asked Michael, his teeth bared. "Explain what this is all about if you know so much."

"Ok, sure. Time's running out. Heheh. That's funny. Look. I'm gonna break it to you, bro, 'cause there ain't no other way to say it. You're me."

They stopped, and Mike held the locket out between them in his fist.

"I don't know how or why, but you are me. Just

look at me. Don't I look familiar, kind of like a family member at a reunion who looks familiar but you just can't place it? Dude, I'm you. Just you in twenty years or so… or possibly more."

They continued on silently, Michael holding Kalila, helping her along, and soon they darted down a back alley behind main street, and Mike was trying the door handle on a small compact car. There was a sound of a revving engine somewhere close and the screeching of tires.

Mike, startled, looked toward the noise and then righted himself and began looking around on the ground to find a chunk of broken concrete which he used to break the window on the car and unlock the door.

"C'mon," said Mike calmly, almost too calmly. "I'll hotwire this bad boy and we'll see how far we can get."

"Before what? Look. I'll grant that we sort of look alike, but, really. I'm you?"

"When I show you, you'll believe. Just get in."

Mike hopped in the driver's seat and reached across to unlock the doors, then proceeded to reach under the dash, yank some wires out, and after sparking them together the engine roared to life.

Mike giggled gleefully.

"Couldn't do this anymore where I was from. No more keys."

Michael helped Kalila into the back seat where she lay down immediately, and he climbed into the passenger seat, slammed the door, and they roared down the alley.

"I know this all sounds weird," said Mike. "Really I do. But dude, look at this scar on my arm."

He rolled up one sleeve while driving with his knee, and there on the inside of his bicep was a jagged scar.

"I guess you got it still. Happened one night when we was twenty-two. Put our arm through a plate glass window and nearly bled to death."

Michael's eyes opened wide and his breathing became thick and heavy. He rolled up his sleeve to reveal the same scar.

"Losing your hair, too. Yeah, we end up homeless after we fail out of every job we have. Life sucks, bro."

Michael stared out the window as they rolled down toward main street. A man was stopping his car in the middle of the street to get out and look at the smashed rear bumper of his compact car.

"But why? How? Why didn't I recognize you before?"

"I don't know. They did something to our memories, made us not know each other. All's I know is that this town is phony right down to the foundation. Whoever's doing all this has yet to show his or her face. Now let's go down under this town and find out what they're up to, huh? Ain't got nothing to lose anyway. Maybe we can make a difference. Stop them before they invade Earth."

Michael looked behind him to check on Kalila, and she was lying in the back seat, possibly asleep, possibly dead. He touched her hand and it was still warm. He hoped she would wake and see him, that they could remake their lives, but his hopes were a shade of the truth, borne along by gossamer wings of tissue and the rain falling from the sky was made of hard nails.

36: Delete

Danny awoke to the sound of Kallie's voice, not really words but the soft groaning of someone in pain. He had something on his face, and when he opened his eyes he realized that the two of them had been encased in a strange shroud of thick foam.

They were suspended near the roof of the car, and he was thankful that he had pulled her toward him during the accident or he might not find her in the springy mess. He began to wriggle free, pulling on Kallie's arm as he did, keeping her close to him, and as he did she slowly woke and started moving more on her own.

Soon they had climbed out of the car, the foam somehow not adhesive, and lay on the dead yellow grass, the car's wheels still rotating slowly, something green pouring from the front of the car. Danny stood and pulled her to him and her face was a blank mask of shock. He left her for a moment to push through the foam, reach inside the door of the car and pull the trunk latch. There was a loud rattle as several items fell out of the trunk to the pavement, and then he ran around to the back of the car to grab a tire iron.

"What...where are we?" Kallie asked, sitting up,

bits of the strange foam clinging to her red hair.

"Don't know. Gotta get out of here. Your dad's still after us."

"He's not my dad…at least I don't think…"

He tried to grin at her, but it registered as an odd smirk.

"C'mon. Let's go. If you see your dad, close your ears again. He seems to have some code he speaks to you that makes you forget."

She looked at him as if in a trance.

"Ok."

They ran back toward the town, but just as they topped the hill there was the sound of a revving engine behind them and the sheriff was bearing down on them, his tires screeching and smoking as he slammed on the brake, and in moments he was stepping out of the car, his head and chest clearly visible above the roof of the Ford Taurus.

"You just need to come with me, now Danny," he roared. "Ain't no use in prolonging this. I don't mean you any harm at all."

Danny grabbed Kallie's hand and they ran down the road, in his frightened condition hoping that he could run away, put as much distance between himself and the horror that was this monster law man.

And then he heard the numbers.

"Two-seven-three-six-

"Kallie hold your ears!"

But it was too late. She stood still as a statue, her arms at her sides, her eyes glassy and non-respondent, and Danny began to shake her, screaming at her to wake up, but she would not.

He wept, pulling at her hand but she would not budge, would not move. She fell completely under the control of the sheriff. And then the monster opened his mouth and out came a strange sound, like the skipping of a record player, a scratching on vinyl, and Kallie fell to the ground, a beautiful rag doll.

"Now come with me before something else happens. I'll make it all go away and you can go back to playing baseball."

Danny's eyes filled with tears and his face tightened, his fist balling up tight around the cold metal tire iron.

"I'll kill you, you merked up freak!"

And he ran toward the sheriff, the tire iron raised above his head, and the sheriff stepped toward him, hands raised as if in defense, but Danny dropped down, sliding as if going in for a home plate score, striking the sheriff just under the kneecap.

Something crunched.

The sheriff did not cry out, but reached down for Danny with a strange agility for such a large man, grabbing him around the chest and lifting him high in the air. Danny swung again, his feet pinwheeling, striking the lawman across the jaw, dislocating it so that the teeth in his mouth angled to the right, but it did not cause him to release his grip. Blood and spittle drooled down the sheriff's lip.

"Just calm down, Danny," he slurred, spitting fluid at Danny. "We'll get you fixed up in a jiffy, don't you worry."

Danny swung again, this time straight through the large cowboy hat, crushing the top of it in the middle, and then Danny was released, dropping to the ground as the big man fell to his knees, then back to a sitting position and then toppling to the side nearly dragging Danny with him.

Danny stood, pulling away from the strong hands, breathing hard, his shoulders rising and falling, and then he looked behind him at the motionless form of Kallie lying in the road. He ran to her, taking her hand but feeling the cold clammy skin, the pulse that was not there.

She was not breathing.

Frantically he did what he had seen in the movies, laying her out on her back and holding back her head while opening her mouth and then breathing into it. He put his hands on her breastbone and pressed. One-two-three-four-one-two-three-four. He could hear something crack inside and it frightened him, caused him to cry out, and then he breathed into her mouth again.

She coughed, moaned, and coughed again, and then her eyes opened, but one of them had blood oozing from it like strange red tears.

"Danny?" she gasped. "My chest hurts."

He laughed loudly, madly.

"Yeah," he said. "I guess it does. Sorry to get handsy."

"What?"

"C'mon," he said, taking her hand and helping her up. "Let's go. I gotta find my mom."

37: Processor

Their car rolled to a stop near the intersection where Michael had seen the disfigured scientist, and as if to prove that what he had seen was not a dream, the manhole cover was lying just to the left of the entrance to the sewer system.

"Ever wonder why such a small town would need so many dang manholes?" asked Mike, shutting off the engine and opening the door. "Course that ain't the half of it. Come with me."

Michael and his older self climbed out of the car, but Michael opened the back door to find Kalila quiet, motionless, her eyes open and staring, one eye full of blood.

"Kalila," he said, climbing in and shaking her, and then he thought about what he called her when they knew each other so many years ago. "Kallie wake up!"

But no answer, no movement, and her skin was cold and clammy.

"You comin'?" asked Mike matter-of-factly. "She ain't real, you know."

Michael stood up out of the car and put a hand on the roof.

"What? She looks pretty real to me."

Mike put his hands on his hips and bent forward at the waist.

"Get over it, bro. She's not real. It's all part of how they are going to take over. Replace us with fakes so that they can control things. They just haven't got the kinks worked out and we're the guinea pigs. We gotta do something, make them hate us or reconsider. Make 'em think we ain't worth the trouble. Fly in the ointment, man!"

Michael's eyes began to water, but the scar on Mike's arm was proof enough even though lying in the car was Kalila Steren, the woman whom he wronged, and he wasn't about to leave her in this car, simulated or not.

"Help me take her with us," Michael said.

"No."

"I'll carry her. C'mon, man."

Mike walked calmly over to Michael and put a hand on his shoulder.

"You gotta leave this in the past where it belongs," he said, his haggard face drawn down. "She was a mistake we made is all. Ain't no going back. Ain't no redoing the past. They took us because they didn't think we'd matter or be missed. Well we gotta show them that no man's life is worthless. We can make a difference for once. Save Earth."

Mike reached into the car again to touch Kalila's cold wrist, resigning himself to the fact that she, Kallie, was indeed not breathing, and followed his older self down the manhole into the darkness. As they neared the bottom of the shaft they were greeted by an eerie green light that illuminated a seemingly endless hallway and cast strange shadows on the pipes and tubing that lined the walls.

"Let's see what we can find," said Mike.

"You mean you don't know where you are?"

"Not really. But let's see what we can tear up."

They began walking, listening to their shoes click on the smooth floors, and this place did not look anything like a sewer system. There was a faint odor of rotten eggs and something like vinegar, and as they walked further and further down the hallway the fumes became stronger, so much that they pulled their shirts up over their noses and held their hands over their mouths.

Mike began to cough.

"You ok?" Michael choked through the fumes. "What the heck *is* this?"

"Haven't a clue," Mike wheezed. "But we gotta find a door or an end to this hall pretty soon if we're gonna make it. Can't take much more of this."

In the distance the long hallway emptied into a dark area, a black cloud of nothing, the emerald light from the hallway falling into it like a black hole in space. They picked up the pace, their footfalls growing louder as they ran, and the gloom of the space in front of them was not growing any lighter, pulling in all of the ambient light, the steamy heat of the air growing more and more dry, cold and silent.

They both stopped just at the edge of the empty darkness, fearful of tripping over something in there. Mike's breathing became a steady whistle of overworked lungs as he leaned against the network of pipes that ran along the walls. Michael pointed into the black.

"In there?" he coughed.

Mike did not answer, only stumbled forward, and Michael after him, following him into the cold darkness.

The two men couldn't hear it, but a faint, high pitched sound began to emanate from every telephone speaker, radio and emergency alert tower in town. Everywhere above ground people began to exit their homes and wander the streets, all of them moving toward a pre-determined destination.

38: Bot

The steering wheel of the Taurus wobbled in Danny's hands as he drove slowly back toward town. Kallie sat next to him, her hands in her lap, biting her lower lip.

"What do we do?" she asked.

"I don't know," Danny responded. "I'm kind of making this up as I go along."

They peaked the last hill before seeing the Sonic drive-in, the Pizza Hut and Super C Grocery, all laid out along the main road leading into town, but there were people everywhere, all of them walking slowly along in one direction, many of them wandering along the middle of the road. There were so many people that Danny had to slow down and drive around them.

People stood swaying back and forth as they walked, their eyes blank and their mouths agape. Danny saw Coach Wood walking down the sidewalk dragging a coat loosely in one hand and a sandwich in the other. Mr. DeForest was wandering near the yellow stripe in the middle of the road, his feet shuffling along, wearing only a pair of boxers. As they passed him they noticed a tooth brush jutting out from his mouth.

And there was a noise. Some kind of noise was faintly heard like that of a tornado siren on Saturday at noon so common in Oklahoma. Danny could hear it faintly, and it caused Kallie to grab his arm.

"What is that sound?" she asked blankly. "I think I need to roll down my window and listen to it."

Danny, his focus trained on not running over the friends and neighbors of his home town, turned to look at Kallie and his eyes grew wide. She was reaching for the door handle, but everything in him told him to stop her.

"Kallie!" he shouted, and she started, pulling back her hand. "Don't get out of the car. We're still moving. There's something wrong with these people and somehow sound has something to do with it. Look what the sheriff did to you."

"Oh yeah," she said, her face blank and unresponsive. "Dad...sheriff."

They rolled along slowly, weaving around pedestrian after trancelike pedestrian, all of them seemingly caught in whatever condition they were in at the time the strange sound began. They wandered, but in a generalized direction that was more unified than random. Danny turned left at a flashing red street light and then right down a side street where people were coming out of their homes and moving toward intersections where several of them were lining up or rather crowding around something in the middle of the street. As he approached he saw a car sitting vacant, its back door wide open but no one inside, and since the crowds of people were becoming more and more thick, making their way impassable, he stopped the car and threw it into reverse.

Kallie opened the door.

"No!" Danny screamed. "Kallie don't!"

It was too late. She stepped out of the car and into the street, leaving the car door open to allow Danny to watch her join the others in their trancelike state, and the sound was louder now, a sonic hiss of static that pulsed in a pattern that was unknown to him, a pattern that was strangely mathematical.

His stomach rolled and he bolted from the car, running around the front to face Kallie who walked toward the crowd of people, and grabbed her by the shoulders. He shook her but she did not flinch, did not make a sound, only stared past him slack jawed, her eyes dull orbs of lifelessness, one of them now oozing blood.

"Kallie!" he shouted, one hand caressing her cheek. "Kallie wake up!"

She moved forward, pushing against him but not

strong enough to push past him, her will bent on following whatever clarion call could be heard in the air around them. He turned, noticing that the people were descending into something in the center of the mob, silently climbing down a ladder in the street, the manhole cover removed and lying discarded on the pavement, and he saw the unmistakable blank stare of his mother in the crowd.

He started toward her, but then he heard a familiar deep voice from behind him.

"Just calm down Danny," said the sheriff, his face a ruin, his hat removed to reveal a deep gash across his matted scalp. "Everything will be okay if you come with me."

And he had left the tire iron in the car.

39: System Failure

Before Danny could breathe, the sheriff's heavy hand was on his shoulder. The grip was inhuman, a cold piece of steel. Danny shifted his weight, trying to break free, reaching for the big man's wrist, but couldn't get his hand around it.

He was being dragged now, away from the mass of people, his mother, and Kallie, who for whatever reason were both ignoring his screams as he struggled desperately against the sheriff.

"Just calm down, now," the lawman repeated, a slight back of the jaw lisp in his voice. "Everything will be fine."

"Let me go!" shouted Danny, working to pry the man's fingers from his shirt, his legs kicking and flailing. "I swear I'll kill you! Let me go!"

The sheriff only repeated the mantra in his strange monotone voice, and Danny finally managed to reach out with all of his might and grab at the legs of a man near him, one of the many people wandering mindlessly toward the hole in the street. At first the man tried to move, but fell to the ground as if he were a toppled mannequin, and Danny held on tightly, digging his fingers into the flesh of this human anchor.

Sheriff Norris continued to drag them both, but Danny was able to use the leverage of the new baggage to swing his legs around and kick at the damaged knee of the sheriff, and this toppled them all to the ground. Danny jumped up, now released from the lawman's grasp, and used the opportunity to stomp the back of the sheriff's head, driving his face into the pavement. Immediately, he ran toward Kallie and his mother, looking through the throng of people who staggered toward the hole.

They had gone, descending into the blackness far below the street, and he was bound to follow them.

40: Reboot

Danny followed the somnambulant crowd as they climbed down the manhole, slowly descending into the darkness.

"Kallie!" he shouted, the echo of his voice pounding his ears. "Mom, where are you?"

The people around him did not speak, only the metallic ping of their shoes descending along the rebar rungs.

He heard a grunt far above him, and when he looked he saw a man being pulled from the hole, tossed out of view above ground like a submissive rag doll, and the twisted face of the sheriff staring down at him, his eyes dripping blood. The slow moving man below Danny who wore scrubs and had a high and tight haircut was not speeding up the pace at all, completely oblivious to the threat from above them.

"It's ok, Danny," croaked the sheriff, his broken jaw causing a deep lisp. "I'll be down there in a second and we'll sort all this out."

Danny climbed down, not wanting to hurt the man below him, but squeezed on past him, and the man in the blue scrubs did not mind apparently, allowing him by. Danny reached the bottom of the shaft where he found the crowd moving down a dimly lit hallway toward a large dim chamber. As soon as Danny's feet hit the floor he was pushing through the crowd looking for Kallie, for his mother. He saw a red pony tail just a short distance ahead and called Kallie's name, but the person did not turn, did not flinch. He pushed further in, squirming past people seemingly oblivious to his presence, and soon he was within arms reach, and that was when he noticed the egg shaped metallic pods sitting in neat rows, filling the massive room as far as he could see.

People were lying down inside of them, the door would close on them, a faint hum could be heard, and then the people stopped moving, eyes closed, no fogging of the glass canopy above their faces.

Danny's mind began to flood with horrifying images as he reached for the red head with the pony tail.

"Kallie!" he screamed. "Kallie please listen to me!"

A woman turned, a bit older than Kallie, but it was not Kallie, and she somehow looked like his mother but more like a distant relative of hers. Danny pushed further, shoving people aside, none of them protesting his violent jostling, and out of the darkness above him came three orb shaped metallic objects, each of them ringed by a halo of yellow energy, each of them with three distinct tentacle shaped arms each tipped with a three fingered appendage.

And they were moving toward him.

Danny couldn't stop, tried to ignore the odd orbs as they descended making strange chirping noises faintly reminiscent of songbirds, and there was a faint sound of whirring as their arms whirled about them. He had to find Kallie. Had to find his mother.

Behind him he heard the deep lisping voice of the sheriff and turned to see the monster pushing his way through the crowd of mindless townsfolk.

"Danny!" he growled. "Danny you have to come with me! This is not according to plan. You were not authorized to see this. It is not time."

Danny turned, pushing further, until he saw the unmistakable curve of Kallie's jawline as she walked slowly toward one of the pods.

"Kallie!" he screamed, but she would not turn, and the transparent hatch of the pod opened, beckoning her within like some horrible pitcher plant.

He pushed past many other people, wading through the sea of unresponsive people, knocking a few of them to the ground in true football fashion, yet none of them protested, only standing again to their feet to move toward their individually assigned pods. He came within inches of her, and she had already placed one foot inside the pod. With every ounce of strength he had left he wrested her free, cradling her in his arms and sinking to his knees with her, sitting on the floor between two of the pods. Large pulsing hoses, some of them looking organic to him, lay quivering on the floor connecting all of the pods together in a huge framework that Danny did not understand.

"Danny!" screamed the sheriff, his head visible above the crowd, but Danny was not moving, could not move, exhausted from the fight through the crowd.

Kallie lay in his arms, her eyes closed, her breathing erratic, and he could feel her heartbeat as he placed one hand just under her throat. He could hear the heavy, scraping footfalls of the sheriff as he approached through the crowd, shoving people out of his way as he went with super-human strength, but Danny would not leave her, and he lay her on the floor, stood, balled up his fists, and readied himself for a fight.

The last person between Danny and the sheriff, a middle aged man wearing a Foo Fighters concert t-shirt, was jerked aside and thrown down, lying motionless as the sheriff stood before him, his jaw off kilter, his red eyes oozing, a stream of red blood flowing down from his forehead.

"You have to come with me," he said, and Danny braced himself to fight, but cable-like arms wrapped around the sheriff's limbs and neck and the terrifying lawman began to rise above the crowd into the darkness as the clicking whirring orbs seized him. The big man fought against them, his broken shades falling from his pocket to the black floor at Danny's feet, and the sheriff's grunts could be heard as he disappeared into the darkness above.

"Danny?" said Kallie behind him, her faint voice almost a whisper. "You really must stop."

He spun to face her, and as the multitude of people climbed into their individual pods he stood staring at her lovely face, yet her eyes were now shedding crimson tears.

He reached for her, took her in his arms and kissed her lips, but they were cold and lifeless.

"Danny," she said, her voice quivering. "You have to stop. The experiment is over and now we have to be redacted."

"What do you mean?" he said, his eyes filling with tears, his lungs filling with acrid air that was somehow not of earth, a smell of sulphur and ammonia.

"I can't explain. The controller will explain," she stammered, her hands taking his, raising them to caress his hand against her blood smeared cheek. She reached for the locket she wore around her neck, broke it loose and weakly put it into his trembling hand.

"I love you, Danny," she whispered, her mouth trying to smile. "I have always loved you. I can't do anything else, was designed to do only that. Please forgive me. I didn't…until now at least…understand why, but now I do. Go see the controller. He calls you now, but my purpose has been served. Please understand. I can't stay awake any longer."

Then she fell away, her eyes drooping, her body falling limp, and he held her tight to his chest for a moment, feeling her heart slow and then cease, and then he cradled her, his sobs deep and full of anguish. He brushed a wisp of red hair from her forehead, kissed her there, and laid her inside the pod gently and stood back to watch the transparent lid close on her, separating them forever.

He lay there in the gloom against the pod for some time, his sobs echoing around the chamber, and then he saw a band of light that ebbed on a far wall, pulsing from left to right, and two figures standing in front of it, both of them the same height.

Standing weakly, he navigated around the pods, trying not to trip on the strange umbilical cables that lined the floor, and made his way over to the two figures, their shadows cast against the floor by the yellow line of light that radiated down a tunnel that he hadn't noticed until now.

One of the men turned, and he recognized him right away, the man who washed dishes at Kendall's.

"Hey, Danny," he said, his face looking all too familiar, as if they were related somehow. "You ok?"

Danny ignored the comment. "What is all this?"

"I don't know," said Michael. "But I think this tunnel might have some answers. Let's go."

Without a word, the three of them ventured into the darkness of the tunnel, the only light the yellow pulsating line that shot down through the void.

And the air tasted stale.

41: Flowchart

Danny, Michael and Mike cast long, pulsating
shadows on the wall as they followed the yellow line
of light down the tunnel, passing ports that spewed
strange steam that left an oily residue on their fingers
as they felt along the walls. The hoses and tubes
became more plentiful as they went, so that they had
to step over many of them, some of them looking as
though they were covered in a hard scaly organic
matter that oozed a thick fluid.

At the end of the tunnel they found a large round
doorway, and a flickering barrier of yellow light was
its only door which hummed and chattered with a
sound of intermittent static. The air became more and
more stale as they went, and they noticed a metallic
taste on their tongues that made them smack and lick
their lips to get rid of it.

Cautiously, they stepped through the light barrier,
feeling a tingle on their skin with each flash of light,
but no harm came to them. They found themselves in
a chamber the size of a modest home, and sitting in
the middle of this chamber was a large spherical pod
with yellowed windows, and a large spiny black
creature as big as a car swimming in a liquid within,

some of its spines floating listlessly behind the glass.

"What is that?" asked Mike, reaching out to touch the glass.

It moved, and he reflexively pulled his hand back. It looked to Michael like a giant sea urchin, but some of its skin had peeled away, exposing a bluish flesh beneath.

A bluish holographic screen switched on to their left and a chatter of clicks and whistles caused them to grit their teeth, the sound of it rattling the chamber walls. All of them put their hands over their ears to drown it out and could not, but soon it subsided, and the thing in the tank dropped to the bottom so that they could all see its black spiny top.

"Hey, there's writing on this thing," said Michael, waving his hand through the holographic image as it stuttered and sparked.

"What does it say?" Danny asked.

Mike bent close to it.

< Welcome.>

"Do you think that thing is talking to us?" Danny asked.

The three of them moved closer together, and Michael put his arm around Danny. The screen flickered, the room suddenly lit only by the yellow light coming from the holding tank, and then it flickered back to life again.

They read the screen.

<It is a pleasure to finally communicate with you. Our apologies for the ordeal you have been forced to endure. It is a sad mistake that we have committed, and we will be solving the problem momentarily.>

"That's right you will!" screamed Mike, breaking away from the two others. "I've been through hell. Well, you won't get away with this. Humans won't be slaves to your planet. We'll figure out a way to stop you from taking over!"

<I am sorry you feel that way. It is not our intention to subjugate your species. Apparently you have thapslke us.>

"What?" asked Michael. "That last part was garbled."

<Again, I am sorry. Apparently our translator is also malfunctioning due to the space-time oversight. Please... do not...misunderstand...us. We meant no harm. We simply thought, sadly, that you would not be missed since you did not affect your environment. We only meant to study you. I will try to explain, but my time is short, and I must act soon to right our mistake.>

"Mistake?" asked Danny. "What mistake?"

<We transported you from your time stream in three different periods of your life. First, subject three, shortly before the time of your death under a cross portal due to

cold temperatures, second , subject two, when you were in the middle of your life, and finally, subject one, at the start of your life. This, so we thought, would avoid any space-time anomalies. We could only transport one entity given the 7599j/s994905993(root) equation, but we needed to see how humans interacted. We constructed the town above based on extensive study and replicated the populous from genetic matter available.>

Michael sat on the floor, his hands grasping his knees. Danny turned away from the screen, his eyes filling with tears. Mike clasped his hands behind his back and stared at the flickering holographic screen.

"You mean, none of them were real?" asked Michael, subject two. "Kalila?"

"Told ya," said Mike, subject three, his face drawn down.

<Yes. The entity you knew as Kalila, sub-designate Kallie, was placed in the town to interact, programmed with the memories you have of her. I am sorry she malfunctioned. The space-time anomaly corrupted the environment, having adverse effects on the simulated populous, including the minder we placed in the environment to keep you safe. He has been recycled as were all of the other simulations.>

"Recycled?" Danny said, standing and spinning to face the thing in the tank. "You mean Kallie?"

<Yes. I apologize. In our study of humans we did not factor the emotional attachments that you place on others. However, the space-time anomaly is more destructive than we ever imagined. This is a failed experiment, but we must try to right what we have done before more damage is irreparably s;icm;oak. It has caused much damage, and I am the last of my team as the rest of them have succumbed to the effects of the anomaly. I do not have long. It is very...destructive. And you are all in danger.>

"So you are going to, what, recycle us?" asked Danny.

Michael put a hand on Danny's shoulder.

<In a sense. Due to the space-time anomaly, we will only be able to send one of you back. You will appear exactly in the point of origin from which you were taken. However, this must be the youngest form, subject one, designated as "Danny". You will not remember any of this if our 40298j8s9fa' are correct. You have a matter of thirty minutes your time to speak to one another, to... discuss emotional attachments... 92;lkdja;9 Then, subject one, designate "Danny" must enter the time chamber at precisely ;9029j;,vc9eea;&& to be sent back to his exact moment of departure.>

To the left of the holographic screen, descending out of the darkness of the ceiling, a silver orb floated to the floor. A red line of light appeared on the top, bisecting the orb vertically, emitting a loud humming sound, until it divided the side facing them to reveal a hollow center that pulsed with a strange red glow. The strange steam began to flow out of the pipes in the walls, collecting on the floor in a soft haze of thick crimson fog.

"What do we do?" asked Mike, turning to face them, his eyes welling with tears. "I don't want to die here."

"We don't have a choice, apparently," said Danny, his face wan and reserved. "So our lives...my life... didn't matter enough to be missed by the people around me?"

All three of them stood facing one another, Danny's words hanging heavy in the air between them, so thick it could almost be seen through the gloom.

"We have to make it right," said Mike. "I don't want to die under a bridge in the cold. We have to get you to remember this, you know, when you go back. We have to get you to make our life right."

"How?"

They stood silent for a bit, and then Michael noticed something shiny hanging from Danny's closed fist.

"What is that?"

Danny raised it up and held it in his hand, let it dangle between them.

"It's Kallie's locket," he said, his eyes watering again. "I...she gave it to me just before she..."

"Dude, she wasn't real," said Mike. "Get over it. Life is hard. You take it on the chin."

"Shut up!" screamed Danny. "You don't get to make statements here. You screwed it up. This is all because of what you did, because of what you both did, because of what I might do."

Michael stood between them, placing a gentle hand on each shoulder.

"It doesn't have to be this way," Michael said. "It all has to do with the prom. That night. What happened there. If things were different, we could have a chance, not go through this. Not have to be taken."

There was silence, and Mike began to nod.

"Yeah," said the old man. "Not have to be taken. Reset everything."

Michael opened the locket with trembling fingers and within he found the picture of Kalila, but she was much younger, much happier, before the night when he saw her only as an object, and not as a sweet, loving girl, a girl with hopes and dreams and a good life that they could have shared together. He closed

it, placed it back in Danny's hand, and gripped
Danny's shoulder with hard fingers.

"You have to remember, Danny," said Michael.
"You have to remember not to go to the lake with
Kallie. Don't go on that drive."

"But he...it... said I wouldn't remember anything.
What if I repeat what you did, what we did? What if
it doesn't work?"

"It has to," said Mike. "It has to work. Just
believe that it will."

Danny squeezed the locket as if it were some type
of magic charm, opened it up one more time to see
her face, the face that he watched slip away from him,
go slack, and drift off to death. He would have her
back. He had to. He must. And he would treat her
with respect, not see her as an object, a thing to be
possessed. She was lovely, a beautiful person who
just wanted to love him. Just wanted to be his love.

The orb began to hum louder, and Danny stepped
cautiously forward, reaching out with one fist which
held the locket as if to block the harsh red light that
was growing in intensity from the center of the orb,
the red lightening whipping out of it, searching,
probing like tentacles around the walls of the room.
He put his foot inside, feeling a tingling sensation on
his skin, and then he fell inside of it as it grabbed him,

and everything went black.

Epilogue

"I didn't know you could dance like that," she laughed as he helped her into the Mustang, her sparkling blue dress reflecting the streetlamp light in tiny dazzling stars.

"Me either," he said as he closed the door and jogged around the car, the bow tie of his tuxedo loosened and flapping in the quiet spring breeze.

She waited, turning the rear view mirror toward her to check on her makeup, but she didn't need to. She was radiant. Her shining red hair up and curled, the small dash of glitter still remaining on her soft skin. She hoped her deodorant was still working.

He opened the door, climbing inside, and before buckling his seat belt he leaned over for a kiss which she readily provided, placing a cool hand on his cheek as she did.

"Where to now?" she asked.

He reached into his pocket to find his keys and found something else, a small chain, and when he pulled it out he stared briefly at the shining silver locket that dangled there.

He smiled, looked at her, looked back at the locket.

"My locket?" she said. "I've been looking all over

for that. You had it?"

"Yeah, apparently," he replied, handing it back to her. "Was in my pocket the whole time."

She put it around her neck, then frowned.

"The clasp is broken," she said, and then held it out in front of her, watching it glisten in the dome light of the car.

"Easily fixed," he replied, shooting her a smile. "Tomorrow we can go over to the Walmart and get another chain."

She shrugged, and when she did, he thought about how much he loved her, not the picture of her in the locket, but the real her, the Kallie that was his true friend, his best friend, and how wonderful she was to him.

"Hey," he said, taking a deep breath. He paused for a moment before speaking, watching her eyes sparkle. "Let's not drive out to the lake like we planned. I think my mom would like to have some pictures of us. Didn't really get to do that. Kind of important to her. Wanna go to my house? Watch movies?"

"As long as you have food," she said. "No way am I eating from a fondue fountain. That was gross."

They laughed as he put the car in gear and pulled out of the parking lot of the Embassy Suites. It would be a short drive home to Noble, and his mother would appreciate their company.

Other novels by Roger Colby:

This Broken Earth, 2011
The Transgression Box, 2009
FIVE RIMS TRILOGY
The Terminarch Plot, 2016
The Terminarch War, 2017
The Shibboleth Code, 2018

Roger Colby is an English teacher by trade, making the lives of teens in his class difficult yet rewarding even if they cannot see the use for the important skills he is teaching them (for the most part). He is a father of four rambunctious children and is husband to a wonderful, beautiful, understanding wife who gives him space to write about weird places and even weirder happenstances. He has many dogs, cats, chickens, and birds.

It is a noisy house.

www.ingramcontent.com/pod-product-compliance
Lightning Source LLC
Chambersburg PA
CBHW072213170626
46813CB00003B/914